# THE
# NOBODY
# CLUB

MADGE HARRAH started her writing career as a playwright, studying with the late Rod Serling. She has had several one-act plays published, along with four novels for adults, but this is her first novel for young people. Ms. Harrah was, for several years, a women's gymnastics judge in New Mexico and still puts together floor routine music tapes for gymnasts in the area. She is also a commercial artist and has illustrated children's books. As a member of the National League of American Penwomen, she is one of less than twenty members in the nation, out of a total membership of over seven thousand, to qualify in all three categories: Letters, Music, and Art.

She and her husband Larry, a physical chemist, live near the Sandia Mountains in Albuquerque, New Mexico. The couple's two children, Meghan and Eric, now grown, also live in the area.

# THE NOBODY CLUB

## Madge Harrah

AN AVON  CAMELOT BOOK

THE NOBODY CLUB is an original publication of Avon Books. This work has never before appeared in book form.

AVON BOOKS
A division of
The Hearst Corporation
105 Madison Avenue
New York, New York 10016

First Avon Camelot Printing: April 1989

CAMELOT TRADEMARK REG. U.S. PAT. OFF. AND IN OTHER COUNTRIES, MARCA REGISTRADA, HECHO EN U.S.A.

Printed in the U.S.A.

OPM   10   9   8   7   6   5   4   3   2   1

To Meghan, my all-time favorite gymnast.
Also to Linda and John Charzuk
and the staff of the Albuquerque Gymnastics School.

# Author's Note

Just as a person talks about going to school, rather than going to *the* school, so do gymnasts sometimes talk about working on beam, or on bars, or on floor, rather than working on *the* beam or *the* bars or *the* floor.

I'm Nobody! Who are you?
Are you Nobody too?

—Emily Dickinson (1861)

# Chapter 1

"In here, quick! Don't let anyone see you!" The voice was Marcy's, hissing through the lilac leaves.

Kim paused in mid-stride, startled by the sound. She started to turn in that direction.

"No, don't look!" Marcy cried. "Make sure the coast is clear."

Quickly Kim knelt in the grass while pretending to tie her shoe. She moved her eyes from side to side, peering through her lashes. Neither her big brother Scott nor Marcy's little sister Joanne were in sight. Rising, she stepped from the path which she usually followed from her backyard to Marcy's. She circled the bushes slowly, sniffing at the purple blossoms while again looking around both yards. Satisfied at last that no one was watching, she ducked between two of the bushes and dropped to the ground, crawling through a tunnel formed by arching branches. Soon she came to the sagging doorway of the old storage shed near the alley which she and Marcy used as their secret hideout. She slipped through the door and stood up, squinting in the dim light which filtered through one dust-covered window.

Marcy came toward her, a shadowy figure in the gloom. Even so, Kim could see that Marcy's plump face was more swollen than usual, as though she'd been crying. Marcy's blue jeans and yellow T-shirt, stretched tight about her body, were smudged with dirt while her limp brown hair drooped about her ears. She looked miserable.

"What's the matter?" Kim asked, taking a step toward her friend. "I thought we were going to meet at your house and take the bus to McDonald's for lunch."

"I can't eat," Marcy said unhappily. "Something awful has happened."

If Marcy couldn't eat, then the something must indeed be awful. Kim felt a flutter of fear in the middle of her stomach. "What is it?"

Marcy shifted from one foot to another. "Do you think I'm fat?" she finally asked.

The question took Kim by surprise. She couldn't come right out and say to her best friend, "Yes, you're fat."

When Kim didn't answer, Marcy shrugged. "You don't have to tell me. All I have to do is look in the mirror to know it's true. Well, guess what?"

That question was easy to answer. "What?"

Marcy's voice dropped to a tragic whisper. "My mom says I have to take gymnastics this summer . . . starting tomorrow. She thinks it'll slim me down."

Kim looked at Marcy's thick legs, two round logs inside the tight jeans. Then she looked at her own legs, extending like long, thin sticks from beneath her shorts. Her knees were so knobby she could see the shape of the bones under the skin. She flinched, remembering

2

how the other girls at school had made fun of her and Marcy during P.E.

"You have to wear a leotard in gymnastics," she stated flatly.

Marcy nodded, her face twisting as though she might cry again. "It'll make me look like an elephant."

Kim felt glad that she wasn't the one who'd have to wear the leotard. "I'm sorry," she said, knowing that the words wouldn't help.

"Then take gymnastics with me. Please, Kim," Marcy begged.

Kim hadn't expected that. "No. I . . . I couldn't. No."

"*Please!* Marcy pleaded. "Don't make me take it alone."

"Marcy, I—no, I just can't," Kim said again.

Guilt flooded through her when she saw the hurt look on Marcy's face. She glanced away, looking around the room at the old card table, the two unmatched chairs, the sagging set of shelves they'd collected that winter to furnish their hideout. And the sign she'd lettered to hang on one wall: THE NOBODY CLUB.

"I thought we were best friends," Marcy said sadly. "You and me. Nobodies."

We sure chose the right name for our club when we picked that, Kim told herself. Two losers, that's what we are.

The two biggest Nobodies in fifth grade the whole past year. A fat Nobody and a skinny Nobody. In leotards. . . .

Picturing that, Kim found that she, too, had lost her appetite. "Can't you talk your mother out of it?"

"I already tried. Threw a fit a while ago. Cried, slammed the door. But she threatened to ground me for the rest of the day, so I had to stop."

"How about asking your father?"

"John's not my father, he's my stepfather."

"But maybe—"

"Besides, John hates me," Marcy interrupted. "He only cares about Joanne. She's his. I'm not."

"He adopted you."

"Mom made him do it."

"Are you sure?"

"Sure I'm sure. When they got married six months ago—well, I knew he didn't want me, I could tell."

Kim pressed her lips together to keep from arguing further. She knew that Marcy's real father had walked out long ago, leaving Marcy's mother to get a divorce, while Mr. Doyle's first wife had been killed in a car wreck, leaving him alone with little Joanne. Kim had thought it was a good thing when Marcy's mother had married the tall, quiet Mr. Doyle, for now Marcy would have a father and Joanne would have a mother, but Marcy didn't see it that way. Kim felt strange whenever she heard Marcy call her new father "John" instead of "Dad."

"Please, Kim," Marcy begged again. "We swore an oath always to stick together, you know that. A *blood* oath." Marcy held out her right hand with the index finger extended. "Don't you remember?"

How could she forget? Kim squeezed her fingers together, shuddering as she felt again the prick of the needle which had brought that welling drop of red. With mingled blood, she and Marcy had sealed the pact to form The Nobody Club. A club with only two members.

**4**

For Kim's brother Scott was Somebody, the star quarterback of his high school football team, and he had girlfriends galore. Even little Joanne, just two years old, was Somebody. With golden curls, big brown eyes, and dimples on either side of a perfect smile, she had won the Beautiful Child Contest held by Dalton's Department Store a few weeks back, and her picture had appeared in the newspaper.

But Kim and Marcy had never won an award, not one, not ever.

"Final registration's this afternoon," Marcy went on. "At the Gymnastics Center, over on Belmont. That's only four blocks away. We can ride our bikes. Come on, Kim, ask your mom."

Kim sighed, knowing that she was bound by their oath to do what Marcy asked.

Together they left the clubhouse and slipped through the tunnel under the bushes. After making sure both yards were still empty, they darted out and rose quickly to their feet, then strolled casually away so no one would suspect about the hideout.

They crossed Kim's patio and entered the kitchen where they found Kim's mother talking on the phone. Even though Kim signaled several times that she had an urgent question to ask, Mrs. Turner only nodded toward her with a vague look in her eyes while murmuring into the receiver, "Uh-huh. Hmmmm. Is that right? Yes. Hmmmm. . . ."

Kim waved her hands and made a face to show her mother that she needed her attention, but Mrs. Turner shook her head while continuing to talk into the phone. At last she said, "Well, I have to go. Kim's here acting

5

like the house is on fire, or something. Okay, see you later. Bye.''

As her mother hung up the phone, Kim burst out, "If the house *had* been on fire, you'd have burned up by now!"

"Don't be impertinent," replied Mrs. Turner sternly. "What is it you want?"

Kim explained.

Mrs. Turner frowned as though she were thinking hard. "Gymnastics? Well, I don't know. How much will it cost?"

"I know how much it is, Mrs. Turner," Marcy put in eagerly. "I heard my mom talking about it with John."

As Marcy proceeded with the details about the enrollment, Mrs. Turner frowned even harder while pulling at her lower lip.

"Well, I guess we could manage that," she said at last. "But don't forget, Kim, you're to help me around the house this summer. If I should go back to work—"

"Oh, Mom, I thought you were going to stay home now!" Kim interrupted in dismay. "When you quit your job this spring, you said—"

"I know, but there's a chance . . . well, we'll talk about it later. Nothing's definite yet." She shrugged and smiled, changing the mood. "Look, I've made a bowl of tuna salad and a pitcher of orange juice, if you girls are hungry."

"Thanks, Mom, but we'd better ride our bikes to the gym and enroll before the classes fill up."

Mrs. Turner reached for her purse on the kitchen counter. "I'll go ahead and write the Gymnastics Center a check, and you can take it with you."

6

While Kim got her bicycle out of the garage, Marcy ran home for her own bike and money. Soon the two girls were on their way to the gym. The trip took only a few minutes. When they reached the long metal building, they locked their bikes to the rack out front, then entered and joined a group of adults and young people already lined up before the registration desk.

"We're the only ones here without our parents," Marcy whispered, sounding a little frightened.

"So? Won't we be in sixth grade next fall? We don't need our parents to lead us around anymore," Kim declared.

Trying to act cool, she casually glanced around the gym. It was a large room with a high ceiling, and it was filled with strange equipment.

"Would you look at all that stuff?" Marcy hissed in her ear. "What do you think it is?"

Whatever it was, it looked dangerous. There was a set of uneven bars on poles, resembling something out of a trapeze act in a circus. Kim had a sudden mental picture of herself hanging by her knees with her face turning purple and her tongue sticking out.

She glanced away from the bars toward a thick leather log resting on metal legs at the end of a runway. She heard someone in line call it a horse.

"If that's a horse, where's its head and tail?" she whispered to Marcy.

"I dunno. What do you do, ride it?"

"Don't ask me." Nearby she saw a long beam of wood bolted to silvery supports that lifted it high off the floor. "We don't have to get up on *that* thing, do we?"

Marcy shook her head to show she didn't know. Kim

turned to survey the huge mat which covered the floor along one end of the room in front of a large mirror. Her nerves jarred with shock when she spotted a red-haired girl in a yellow leotard posing before the mirror: Jay Jay Carr, the snottiest girl last year in fifth grade. Jay Jay. There she stood with her chin in the air and her arms curved above her head like a ballet dancer.

"Don't look now," Kim murmured, poking Marcy in the ribs, "but there's Jay Jay."

Marcy looked at once. "If she's in our class, I'll die!"

Jay Jay pivoted on one toe and lunged, balancing on a deeply bent right leg with her left leg extended at an angle behind her. She did look dramatic, Kim had to admit. Last year Jay Jay had been the star tumbler during P.E., while Kim and Marcy had stumbled around looking like clods. Jay Jay was Somebody and she knew it.

"Oh, no, here she comes!" Marcy wailed. "Pretend you don't see her."

Kim turned away, examining with fake interest a large poster of a gymnast which was hanging on the wall behind the registration desk.

"Hey, Kim! Marcy!" called Jay Jay. "Are you taking gymnastics this summer, too?"

Kim sighed, knowing there was no way out of it. She'd have to say hello. As she turned around, she caught Jay Jay looking her up and down with a glint in her eye.

"You have to wear a leotard, you know," Jay Jay said.

She didn't add that she thought Kim and Marcy were

going to look funny. She didn't have to. The tone of her voice told Kim that's what she meant.

"What class will you be in?" Kim asked, hoping that Jay Jay wouldn't say Beginners.

"Beginners," said Jay Jay, "but only for a while, until they decide where I really belong."

I can tell you where you really belong, Kim thought, but stopped herself from saying the words out loud.

"Well, I'd better go practice my cartwheels," Jay Jay went on, giving them a cool smile. "You have to be able to lead with either arm, and you have to keep your arms and legs straight."

As Jay Jay pranced back to the floor mat, Marcy moaned in Kim's ear, "She *knows* I can't do cartwheels. . . . Oh, no, look at that!"

With her arms and legs flashing, Jay Jay had launched herself into a series of right-handed cartwheels.

"We're doomed," said March gloomily.

"Cheer up. We'll do okay," Kim told her.

But underneath she was scared. She had the feeling that this was going to be the worst summer she'd ever known.

# Chapter 2

Kim groaned as she turned before her bedroom mirror the next morning.

"Black! Why did I choose a black leotard?" she wailed at her reflection.

Her long thin neck, her skinny legs with their knobby knees, reminded her of something she'd seen before. Frowning, she piled her hair on top of her head. That made her neck look even thinner, rising from the V neck of the leotard, while her nose seemed to stick out from her face like a beak.

Then she remembered. Last week she'd seen a picture in *National Geographic* of a long-necked crane with tall skinny legs standing in shallow water in the Everglades.

A bird, she told herself scornfully. I look like a stupid bird!

She and Marcy had bought their leotards at the gym the day before, from a table where used gym clothing was on sale. When they'd sorted through the pile, they'd found there were no pretty colors in their sizes. Kim had chosen this plain black one, while Marcy had bought a bright red one with a round neckline and two broad, white bands across the chest. Once they'd arrived home, Kim had paid Marcy back with the money her grandmother had sent her for her birthday.

Now she cast a desperate glance at the clock: 8:30. Too late to do anything about the leotard now. Their first gymnastics class started at 9:00.

Quickly she pulled shorts and a T-shirt on over the leotard, then slipped into her shoes and hurried to get her bike. She met Marcy in the alley. Marcy was dressed in jeans and a baggy sweatshirt, and her face looked puffy as though she'd been crying again.

"Oh, Kim, I look awful," Marcy gulped. "I've got my leotard on under here, and I look like a red beach ball. I didn't know I was *that* fat."

"Maybe you don't—"

"I do, I look terrible! Mom says I shouldn't have bought a red leotard, that red makes a fat person look even fatter. *Now* she tells me!"

Kim sighed bleakly. "Come on, let's get this over with."

When they arrived at the gym, they found a number of other girls milling around near the desk in front. One of them, a slender girl with black hair, met Kim's eyes and then looked quickly away. Kim nudged Marcy and pointed toward the girl with a slight nod of her head. The girl was new in town and had entered Kim's and Marcy's class only two weeks before school ended. Although Kim knew the girl's name was Lisa Andrelli, she knew nothing else about her, for the girl had neither spoken in class nor tried to make friends. Kim and Marcy had decided she was stuck-up.

12

"First Jay Jay, and now that snobby Lisa!" Marcy whispered. "I'm sure glad you're here with me, Kim."

Looking around then for Jay Jay, Kim spotted her off to one side practicing some dance steps. That day Jay Jay had on a dark blue leotard trimmed with white chevron stripes. Her red hair was pulled back with a blue ribbon, and she had on white socks with blue trim.

"Everything she wears always *matches,*" Marcy moaned. "She makes me sick."

A young man dressed in a blue warm-up suit approached the group.

"Hi, I'm Eric Slater, your coach," he announced. "Just call me Eric. Put your shoes and other things on those shelves over there. Then come out on the floor mat and start jogging laps."

Soon Kim and Marcy were trotting around the mat in a circle, along with the other girls. Kim slid her eyes toward Marcy, watching the bulges jiggle around her waist.

"Sl-slow down," Marcy gasped.

As Kim slowed to keep pace with her friend, Jay Jay came loping past.

"What's the matter, tired already?" she asked with a little laugh. Sprinting ahead, she rose into the air in a high split leap, landed lightly, and ran on again.

"She's just a big show-off," Kim said reassuringly to Marcy. "Don't pay any attention to her."

"She makes me *sick!*" Marcy muttered.

After they had run for about five minutes, Eric called, "Sit down now on the mat for your stretching exercises. If you don't get every muscle warmed up, you can strain something and hurt yourselves."

**13**

He pointed toward a tall, brown-haired girl in a pink leotard. "This is Tish Laughlin. She's on our advanced team here at the gym, and she'll be helping teach your class this summer."

Tish had to be at least sixteen years old, Kim thought. She looked gorgeous in her leotard.

"We'll start with bent-knee sit-ups!" Tish announced, flashing them a smile. "Just follow me."

She lay down on the mat in front of them and bent her knees with her feet resting on the floor. While she led the class in sit-ups, Eric took roll call. He smiled and nodded at each girl as she answered to her name, but Kim wasn't fooled. She saw a cold gleam in his eye which told her that he could get tough if he had to.

After sit-ups, Tish led the class in push-ups. Then they practiced splits in three directions: right, left, and center. Kim could get all the way to the floor on her left splits but not on her right. Center splits seemed impossible. From the corner of her eye, Kim watched Jay Jay split her legs straight out on either side and then lean her body forward, flat onto the mat.

"Good pancake!" Tish called, smiling at Jay Jay.

Kim glanced toward Marcy in despair. Marcy just shook her head.

"Now we'll do bridges," Tish said.

"I know what those are!" Jay Jay said brightly. She rolled over on her back and placed her flattened palms on the floor on either side of her head. She pushed up, arching her back in a horseshoe shape.

"That's a bridge, all right!" Tish said. "Do you see that, class? Bridges teach you how to arch your back so you can do walk-overs."

**14**

"Back walk-over," announced Jay Jay.

She kicked her feet away from the floor and balanced on her hands as her feet traveled over her head to land on the floor behind her. Still keeping her balance, she stood up and stretched her arms above her head.

"That's very good—"

"Jay Jay," said Jay Jay.

"That's very good, Jay Jay. Have you had gymnastics before?"

"Just in P.E. at school," Jay Jay replied, "but the teacher said I have natural talent."

Kim once more glanced toward Marcy. Marcy clutched her stomach and bulged out her cheeks to show she wanted to throw up.

Now Tish led them in doing forward and backward somersaults. Next they did somersaults with legs extended to either side. Tish called them "straddle rolls," but Kim called them torture.

At last, Eric approached the mat and said, "Okay, I think you're warmed up enough now. Time for some cartwheels!"

"Oh, no," Marcy groaned, clutching Kim's hand.

Tish went first, demonstrating how the body should be kept straight with arms and legs angling away like the spokes of a wheel. She did three in a row without stopping.

"Did you see, girls, how she held her arms and legs?" Eric asked. "All right, you . . . Marcy, is it? You go next."

"Don't think about it, just do your best," Kim whispered, giving Marcy's hand a quick squeeze.

Despite her love for her friend, Kim could see that

Marcy looked like an awkward frog as she flopped with bent legs across the mat. When Marcy slipped on the third cartwheel to sprawl in a heap on the floor, Jay Jay giggled out loud. Several other girls began laughing, too. While Tish hurried to help Marcy up, Eric turned toward the girls, and Kim again saw that cold gleam in his eyes.

"Let's get one thing straight right now," he said sternly. "Every one of you is going to look foolish out there on that mat before this summer is over. It's okay to laugh *with* someone, but in this class you will not laugh *at* someone. We're a team here, and we will encourage each other. *Is that clear?*"

Kim decided she never wanted Eric to get mad at her. He was scary when he used that tone of voice. She glanced toward Jay Jay and saw that her face was flushed but her chin was high in the air, as though to say she didn't care she'd been scolded.

"And another thing," Eric went on. "You see that equipment over there? No one—I mean *no one*—gets on the high beam or the uneven bars without a spotter."

Kim wondered what a "spotter" was. She had a sudden picture in her mind of Eric running around the gym with a bucket of paint and a brush, putting spots all over the girls. The thought made her laugh out loud. At once Eric's cold gaze was upon her.

"You think that's funny?" he demanded. "Kim . . . is that your name? Are *you* the one who started all this laughing?"

She could only stare at him in shock with her mouth open.

"A girl who falls off those bars without someone to

**16**

catch her can get hurt," Eric went on. "I repeat, never get on the equipment without a spotter. All right, back to cartwheels."

He marched to the other side of the mat and motioned to one of the other girls to go next. Kim hunched her shoulders and lowered her head in misery. At least she now knew that a spotter was a person who caught the girls if they fell. She felt plump fingers grip her hand and looked sideways into Marcy's sympathetic eyes.

"He's mean," whispered Marcy.

Kim nodded. She thought the class would never end, but at last Eric announced, "That's all for today. This class will meet three times a week, on Mondays, Wednesdays and Fridays, same time as today. Start jogging this weekend, and do your stretching exercises at home so you'll become limber and strong. Don't be surprised if you're sore tomorrow."

With that, he walked away to greet the next class.

As Marcy and Kim pulled their clothes on over their leotards, Marcy whispered, "I don't like him. I don't like him at all."

"He thinks I'm the one who laughed at you," Kim said in despair. "He thinks I'm the troublemaker."

"Who cares what he thinks?" Marcy put her arm around Kim. "I know it was Jay Jay. You're my best friend. You'd never laugh at me."

Remembering how she'd thought Marcy looked like a frog, Kim felt a stab of guilt. She turned to see Lisa standing beside the uneven bars and staring up at the high bar out of shadowed eyes which looked like two dark smudges in the middle of her pale face. She held so tightly to the support pole with one hand that her knuck-

**17**

les showed white. After a moment she left the bars and pushed past Kim without speaking, her face still pale and set in a masklike expression.

"Stuck-up, just like we thought," Marcy murmured.

But that night, while Kim did her exercises before going to bed, she found she could not get Lisa's expression out of her mind. She decided that Lisa had looked less stuck-up than she had looked frightened.

Suddenly it dawned on her that neither she nor Marcy had ever tried to talk to Lisa. They'd waited for Lisa to speak first.

Maybe she's shy. Maybe she's afraid of us, Kim thought. But that seemed ridiculous. After all, she and Marcy were Nobodies. How could they frighten anyone?

And yet Kim felt sure that the girl had been frightened of something. What could it be?

She crawled gingerly into bed, favoring her sore muscles. As she shifted about, searching for a comfortable spot, she told herself that she and Marcy had enough problems of their own without worrying about someone else's.

She fell asleep wishing she'd never heard of gymnastics.

# Chapter 3

The next morning Kim hurried through her Saturday chores. She dusted all the furniture and then began vacuuming the carpets. While she was sweeping her parents' bedroom, she found a magazine on the floor beside her mother's side of the bed. Some words on the cover leapt out at her: FAT OR THIN—WHAT YOU WEAR CAN MAKE THE DIFFERENCE.

She sat down on the edge of the bed and flipped through the magazine until she found the article. She skimmed it quickly, taking in the main points. The colors red, orange, yellow, or white make a person look fatter, while dark blue or black make one look slimmer. A V neck is slimming, but a round neckline is not. A plump person should wear vertical stripes, while a thin person should wear horizontal stripes. As for hair, short fluffy hair with bangs across the forehead will widen a narrow face. Long straight hair parted on the side and pulled back from the forehead will make a round face look thinner.

After reading the article, Kim had an idea which

filled her with growing excitement. When she had finished all her work, she grabbed her leotard and hurried over to Marcy's house.

Two-year-old Joanne opened the door. She still had on her long white nightgown and looked like a tiny angel with her golden curls, despite a smudge of jam on her chin.

"Mawcy's in da baffwoom," she said, motioning down the hallway with one dimpled hand.

Marcy came out at that moment carrying a washcloth.

"Joanie," she called, and then grinned a welcome when she saw Kim. "Hi, I'm babysitting. Mom and John have gone shopping." She came forward and knelt to give Joanne a hug. "You're a cutie, you know that?"

Kim knelt, too. "Marcy, she *is* cute. You do like her, don't you?"

The little girl reached up to pat Marcy's face. "Mawcy nice."

Marcy grinned back. "Joanie, you're a munchkin." She shook her head at Kim. "I always wanted a sister. It's just John I wish would go away."

While Marcy washed Joanne's face, Kim described the article in the magazine.

"We've done everything wrong," she ended. "I should be in red, you should be in black. So I have an idea. Let's switch leotards."

"But yours will be too small for me," Marcy protested.

Kim held up her leotard and pulled at one sleeve. "Maybe not. See how it stretches?"

Marcy's face brightened with sudden hope. "Let's give it a try."

The two girls hurried to Marcy's room with Joanne

tagging along. While Marcy slipped out of her shorts and shirt, Joanne climbed up on the bed and plumped herself down in the middle, watching the others with bright-eyed interest.

"Mawcy take off cwothes?" she asked.

"That's right, hon. I just hope this works."

As Marcy struggled into the leotard, Kim began to fear that the material wouldn't stretch enough. It did, however, and soon Marcy stepped back, modeling for Kim while asking, "What do you think?"

For a moment Kim stood speechless. She couldn't believe that color and style could make so much difference.

"You look so much thinner. I'm not kidding."

"You really think so?"

"Just a minute, let me try something else."

Stepping to the dresser, Kim picked up a comb. She parted Marcy's hair on the side, swirled the whole top section back from Marcy's face and fastened it with a barrette.

Joanne clapped her hands. "Mawcy pwetty!"

"I wouldn't go *that* far," Marcy said dryly.

But when she turned to look at herself in the mirror, she broke into an amazed smile.

"I do look better, I really do!"

Digging into the top drawer of her dresser, she pulled out the red leotard and held it toward Kim.

"Now it's your turn."

Kim's pulse pounded with excitement as she took off her clothes and slipped into the leotard. But when she stepped before the mirror, she let out a groan of disappointment. The leotard hung on her like a wrinkled sack. She glanced toward Marcy's face in the mirror and saw the same disappointment reflected there. Marcy began at once to pull off the black leotard.

"Guess I'd better take this off and give it back before I stretch it any more than I already have."

"Hold it!" Kim said suddenly. "I have another idea."

She skinned out of the red leotard and turned it inside out to read the label in one seam.

"Look, it says to wash this alone in cold water. Maybe if we—"

Marcy nodded eagerly, taking it up. "Maybe if we washed it in hot water, it would shrink."

"Let's go for it."

The two girls put their shorts and shirts back on.

"Come along, Joanie, we're going to do some laundry."

"Wandwy?" Joanne asked. "Me do wandwy!"

Marcy made a face toward Kim. "She wants to do everything I do. It gets to be a real pain sometimes." To Joanne she said, "I'll let you put the leotard in the machine, okay?"

Joanne smiled. "Okay."

In the laundry room, Marcy set the machine's dials for a short cycle with hot water. She held Joanne up and let her drop the leotard into the machine, then closed the lid and started the cycle.

Kim felt a little tickle of fear. What if they ruined the leotard? She'd have to give Marcy the black one if that happened. And she had no money to buy another.

Marcy picked up a tiny pink shorts outfit from the ironing board. "Come on, sweetie," she said to Joanne, "let's get you dressed."

They returned to Marcy's room. While Marcy dressed the little girl and combed the tangles from her golden curls, Kim thought again about the article she'd read. She turned toward the mirror and lifted a section of long hair from the side of her head. She pulled the hair around and spread the ends over her forehead to make bangs.

Hmmmmm, she thought. It really does make my face looked wider.

"Marcy, you got any scissors?"

"In my desk drawer." Marcy glanced over her shoulder. When she saw what Kim was doing, suspicion dawned on her face. "You're not going to cut your hair, are you?"

"I might. What do you think?"

Marcy walked over and studied Kim's face from all angles. "Not bad. Do you really have the nerve?"

Kim took a deep breath. "I—yeah, I'm gonna do it!"

She got the scissors from Marcy's desk. Then she draped a towel around her shoulders and placed another towel on top of the dresser to catch the hair as it fell. She carefully measured out the hair for the bangs, then combed it in a waterfall down over her eyes.

"I can't see. Marcy—"

"Not me!"

"Please, Marcy. Just cut straight across, where my eyebrows are."

"Kim—"

"Come on, it's okay. I trust you."

"But I don't trust me." Nevertheless, Marcy took the scissors. "You're sure?"

"I'm sure."

*Snip, snip.*

The sound sent a shiver down Kim's spine. What was she doing? What would her mother say?

*Snip, snip, snip.*

Enough hair was now gone for Kim to see out of her left eye. "You're not cutting straight."

"Here, you can see now. You do it."

Kim took the scissors. Using one hand to hold the hair in place across her forehead, she cut into the remaining strands.

*Snip, snip.*

The hair fell in yellow clumps onto the towel. Kim's nose tickled, and she sneezed. She still had that shivery feeling, but she felt good, too. When she had finished, she examined herself in the mirror. Her face did look wider. She smoothed the bangs down, then trimmed the ragged edges.

Marcy chewed on her lower lip as she watched. "What'll your mom say?"

Kim giggled nervously. "I don't know, but *I* like it."

There was a dull thud from the laundry room.

"Machine's gone off," Marcy said.

Kim hurried toward the laundry room with Marcy and Joanne following after. She opened the lid on the machine and lifted out the leotard.

"Oh, no! It faded!" Sure enough, the once white stripes were now a bright pink. "So *that's* why the label said wash it in cold water."

The leotard hung in her hands, a limp soggy mess.

"It didn't shrink, either," she added gloomily. "Marcy, I sure am sorry about the stripes."

Marcy sighed. "Look, it's not your fault. Go ahead

**24**

and put it in the dryer. Then come out in the kitchen and we'll have a cookie or something.''

"Cookie!" demanded Joanne.

Marcy shook her head toward Kim with a wry grin. "Didn't I tell you? She copies everything I do.''

They sat at the kitchen table in a pool of golden sunlight which made Joanne's hair glow like a halo. Marcy bit into a chocolate chip cookie, then rolled her eyes toward the ceiling in ecstasy. "I just *love* chocolate!''

"Wuv chockate!" mimicked Joanne.

"There she goes again,'' Marcy said.

But Kim's mind was still on the ruined leotard. "Marcy, I really am sorry about—''

"I told you, it's okay,'' Marcy interrupted. "Actually those stripes are kind of pretty. Don't worry about it.''

Kim searched Marcy's face, hoping she was telling the truth.

"I hate that Jay Jay,'' Marcy went on. "She thinks she's so smart. And that Lisa, too, the way she acts like we aren't even there.''

Kim wanted to tell Marcy she'd thought Lisa might be afraid of them, but today the idea seemed silly. Lisa had looked pretty in her green leotard, and she'd been able to do good cartwheels, too. Why should she be afraid?

When the buzzer on the dryer went off, Marcy hurried to the laundry room. Kim heard the door to the dryer open, and then she heard Marcy let out a yell. "Kim, come quick!''

Kim ran to the laundry room where she saw Marcy holding the leotard out in front of her.

"Look, it's smaller! The heat from the dryer must have done it. Try it on and see."

Again Kim stripped down to her underpants. The leotard felt hot against her bare skin. As she pulled it up over her body, she could tell that it fit much tighter than before. When she had it on she stood back, anxiously watching Marcy's face.

"It's great, Kim! Go look in the mirror."

The two friends hurried to Marcy's room. Stepping before the mirror, Kim looked into the green eyes of a blond-haired girl with bangs dressed in a round-necked red leotard which fit her body like a glove. Even the pink stripes looked good.

"I can't believe it's me!" she cried. She turned to Marcy, whose eyes were dancing.

"Just wait until Monday," Marcy said. "We'll show that Jay Jay a thing or two."

Then Marcy stopped, a worried frown appearing on her face as she glanced around the room. "Where's Joanne?"

Kim had forgotten all about the little girl in her excitement. "I don't know. But it's just been a few minutes—"

"Mom told me never to leave her alone! If something's happened . . ."

Marcy ran out into the hall, calling frantically, "Joanie? Joanie, where are you?"

"In heah," came a small voice from Joanne's room.

"Thank goodness," March breathed. "Mom and John would never forgive me if Joanne got hurt." She hurried into Joanne's room, then let out a shriek. "Oh, no!"

With her heart pounding, Kim ran into the room after

26

Marcy. She saw Joanne sitting in the middle of the floor holding the scissors awkwardly in her small hands. Feathering down over the little girl's shirt and onto the floor fell clumps of golden curls, while the whole top of her head gleamed bald.

"Cut my haiah, too!" she announced with a big smile.

Marcy sank down on the edge of the bed, her eyes wide with horror.

"Oh, Kim," she whispered. "They're gonna kill me."

# Chapter 4

Kim waited until Marcy's parents came home, hoping her presence would keep them from yelling. Marcy met them at the door to try to warn them before they saw Joanne, but just then the little girl came running down the hallway.

"Hi, Mommy!"

Mrs. Doyle let out a shriek. "Oh, no!"

Joanne, who had been fine until that moment, began to wail. She held out her arms to her stepmother, looking pitiful with her bald spot and her face screwed up. There was no doubt about it, Kim thought glumly, Joanne no longer qualified as Dalton Department Store's "Beautiful Child."

Mr. Doyle turned on Marcy, his face stern. "All right, what happened?"

Looking very pale, Marcy stammered out the story.

Mr. Doyle set his mouth in a grim line. "She could have poked an eye out with those scissors, you know."

"I know," Marcy murmured weakly. "John, I'm sorry."

"Saying you're sorry doesn't change things. You should have been more careful."

When Kim saw tears sliding down Marcy's cheeks, she could stand it no longer. "Mr. Doyle, it's—it's not Marcy's fault, it's mine." She was so frightened, looking at his angry face, that her voice trembled. "Joanne watched me cut my hair a while ago. She was copying me."

"Both you girls should have known better than to leave scissors lying around," Mr. Doyle replied, "but Marcy is the one we left in charge. She's the one we hold responsible."

Looking at Marcy's stricken face, Kim wanted to shout, You've said enough! Can't you see how terrible she feels?

Mrs. Doyle picked up Joanne and cradled the sobbing child in her arms. "Marcy, I'm disappointed in you."

"We just can't let this go," Mr. Doyle added. "Marcy, you're grounded for the rest of the weekend. Kim, you'd better go home."

Marcy slid her eyes toward Kim with a look of despair. Kim didn't want to leave her alone, but there was nothing else she could do. Right at that moment she hated Marcy's parents.

She slipped her clothes on over the red leotard and hurried home. She thought how strange it was that life could be so great one minute and so awful the next.

Her own parents surprised her by liking her haircut, but that didn't help much. All weekend she moped around the house, feeling lost without Marcy. Once, on Sunday afternoon when she was sitting on the patio, she saw Marcy come out of the kitchen onto the back steps.

The two girls stared at each other across the broad expanse of their two backyards. Then each one lifted a hand with the three middle fingers pressed together and the thumb and little finger spread out on either side— their secret sign.

Kim ran to the edge of Marcy's yard and called, ''Are you okay?''

Marcy glanced quickly over her shoulder toward the screen door behind her, then came down the steps and moved a little way out into the yard.

''They're still mad at me, and I guess I deserve it. Every time Mom looks at Joanie, she starts to cry, and then Joanie starts to cry, and then John glares at me like I'm a criminal.''

Kim felt a new wave of anger against the Doyles. ''It's not like she's ruined forever. That hair'll grow back.''

''Yeah, I know, but—'' Marcy's voice broke, and she swallowed hard. ''I—I just never seem to do *anything* right. I'm a Nobody for sure.''

''That makes two of us.''

At that moment Mr. Doyle appeared at the screen door. ''Marcy!''

Without another word Marcy turned and hurried back up the steps. Wanting to give Marcy something to look forward to, Kim called, ''Come over and dress at my house for gymnastics tomorrow. I have a surprise for you.''

Marcy waved to show she'd heard, then pushed past Mr. Doyle into the house.

Which left Kim with a problem. She had no surprise. She'd just said that on the spur of the moment. She had no money left, either, even if she could think of something to buy.

As she walked back toward her own house, she wondered if she could make something that would please her friend. Suddenly she remembered what Marcy had said about Jay Jay: *Everything she wears always matches.*

She hurried to the spare bedroom where her mother kept the sewing machine set up. Rummaging around in a box of sewing supplies, she came across a tangle of different colored yarns. Quickly she pulled the fluffy strands apart, letting them fall to the rug in a rainbow-colored shower. Sure enough, she found several black and white strands among the bright colors.

Okay, now what? she wondered.

She remembered the blue edging around Jay Jay's footie-socks. Maybe she could decorate a pair of her own footies for Marcy!

She ran to her bedroom and emptied out her sock drawer. She found one pair of white footies which didn't look too worn and carried them back to the spare bedroom. She got a large darning needle from the sewing box, threaded it with the black yarn, and sewed a decorative edge around the top of one of the socks, using the whip stitch her mother had taught her: over and under, over and under, over and under. When she finished, she slipped the sock onto her own foot. It looked just fine, so she did the other sock, as well. But somehow that didn't seem enough of a surprise. What else could she do for Marcy? Maybe a yarn bow for her hair?

It was then she remembered the yarn pompoms she'd helped her mother make for a clown costume last Halloween. Hoping she still remembered how, she took two strands of yarn, one black, one white, and began looping them together around the extended palm of her left hand. When she had a thick doughnut shape made of the loops, she carefully slipped the yarn from her hand. Grasping the doughnut in the middle, she squeezed it into a figure eight. She wrapped a single strand of black yarn once around the middle where she was squeezing, then tied it as tight as she could. Now she had a black-and-white bow tie. Taking the scissors, she carefully clipped through the loops on either side. When she shook the clipped ends, they fluffed into a pompom. After she had trimmed a few ragged places on the surface of the pompom, she shook it again and then held it out and admired it. She felt proud she'd remembered how.

She made a second pompom. Then, rummaging through her top dresser drawer, she finally found a large, white, plastic barrette. She tied the pompoms to the barrette and snapped the barrette around a lock of her own hair. When she peered into the mirror, she broke into a wide grin, seeing how pretty the pompoms looked. Then she realized how silly she looked, grinning at herself like that, so she crossed her eyes and stuck out her tongue at her reflection.

I'll wrap my gifts, she decided. A present is more fun when it's wrapped.

She took the barrette from her hair and carried it, along with the socks, to the drawer in the kitchen where her mother kept ribbons, tape and wrapping paper. She selected a pretty paper with roses on a white background for her gifts, then topped the package with a shiny red bow.

For a while she felt good, thinking how surprised Marcy was going to be.

But that night she had a nightmare. She dreamed that the big leather vaulting horse turned into a real horse with wild red eyes. When the horse started chasing her, she climbed to the top of the uneven bars to get away. But the bars began to grow like Jack's beanstalk. Soon she found herself pressed against the ceiling of the gym while the horse reared toward her, beating the air with its hooves.

She awoke with a start, her heart pounding.

Go back to sleep, it's only a dream, she told herself. But sleep did not come again for a long time.

# Chapter 5

Marcy knocked on Kim's back door at 8:00 the next morning.

"I couldn't wait," she said when Kim opened the door. "I had to see my surprise."

Kim gulped, feeling a nervous tingle along her arms. Suddenly her present seemed awfully small.

"It—it's just something I made," she said. "It's not very much."

"If you made it, I'll love it. You're my best friend . . ." Marcy's voice caught, and she stopped to swallow hard as though there might be a lump in her throat.

Kim reached out to touch Marcy's arm. "Are your mom and dad still mad?"

"You mean Mom and John," Marcy corrected. "Yes, I guess they are. They've stopped saying much about it, but I can tell." She shrugged, and her face brightened. "Hey, where's that surprise?"

"In my room. Come on."

Kim made Marcy get into her black leotard before handing her the package.

"What pretty paper!" Marcy exclaimed, turning the package over and over in her hands.

"Well, open it!"

Marcy carefully removed the paper, then gasped. "Oh!"

Kim could tell she was truly pleased.

"I told you I'd love it!" Marcy cried. She held up the barrette with pompoms. "Did you really make this?"

"Yes. Put it on."

Marcy parted her hair on the side and combed it back, the way she had on Saturday. She slipped the barrette into her hair and snapped it shut. Then she pulled on the white footies with their black trim. She stepped before the mirror, striking a pose with her arms stretched above her head.

"Everything *matches*," she chuckled. "Just like Jay Jay."

Kim now got into her red leotard. Struck by a sudden idea, she ran to the room with the sewing basket and soon came back with a length of red yarn which she used to tie her hair up in a ponytail.

"Well, I think we look gorgeous," she said. "I wonder if Jay Jay will notice?"

Jay Jay noticed.

When Kim and Marcy took off their shorts and shirts at the gym, Jay Jay began to laugh. Pointing at the red leotard, she said to Marcy, loud enough for the other girls to hear, "You washed it in hot water and it faded, didn't it! Then you shrank it in the dryer and couldn't get it on, and you had to trade with Kim. You're really stupid, you know that?"

Kim felt so angry that she wanted to hit Jay Jay.

Instead, she gave her a shove. "Stop it," she cried. "You're the one who's stupid!"

Eric walked by at that moment. Fixing Kim with a stern frown, he said, "No rough stuff in this gym. Do you hear me, Kim?"

She couldn't believe it. She was in trouble again, and all because of Jay Jay.

"Do you hear me?" Eric repeated.

Jay Jay stood there rubbing her arm and pretending to be hurt while she looked up at Eric with big innocent eyes. It made Kim want to scream. But when she opened her mouth, all that came out was a weak, "Yes, sir."

After Eric moved away, Jay Jay whispered "Ha, ha!" to Kim, and stuck out her tongue.

Kim's stomach churned with frustration. She was afraid Eric would never like her now. Marcy moved close to Kim and squeezed her hand to show her sympathy. Glaring at Jay Jay, she hissed, "You make me sick!"

Jay Jay just smiled and loped forward with the rest of the class to begin jogging around the mat. Sighing in unison, Kim and Marcy followed her. Kim felt as though her footies had turned to lead.

When jogging was over, Tish led the class in their warm-up exercises. Then Eric stepped out onto the mat.

"Today we'll let you try the equipment," he announced. "Before the summer is over, you'll learn simple routines on floor, beam, and bars, and a basic vault over the horse. Then, at the end of the summer, we'll hold a meet, just our class, so you can show what you've learned."

Kim wanted to ask what a meet was, but she didn't have the nerve.

"What's a meet?" asked a black girl farther down the line.

"That's where all of you will perform what you've learned for parents and friends," Eric explained. "We'll have judges who score what you do. The best girls will win ribbons."

"We're doomed," moaned Marcy in Kim's ear.

"All right, we'll try vaulting first," Eric said. "All I want you to do at first is jump on and off the springboard just to get the feel of it. Tish will show you how."

Tish pulled the springboard away from the horse, then trotted lightly to the end of the runway, gave a little jump, sped down the path, and leapt into the air to come down hard on the high part of the springboard. The board bent down under the weight of her body, then snapped back up with a loud pop, flinging her into the air. She flew up and away, landing on her feet a short distance down the runway. She immediately stretched her arms over her head toward the ceiling.

"That's the way you finish a vault," Eric said. "You land on your feet and reach for the ceiling."

"If you don't land on your behind," Kim muttered to Marcy. Marcy just rolled her eyes and shook her head.

Each girl got several tries on the springboard.

"It's not too bad," Marcy finally said. "Kind of like jumping up and down on a bed."

"Okay, Tish, show the girls a squat-over vault," Eric called at last.

Tish pulled the springboard back near the horse. She

**38**

darted to the back of the runway, gave another of those little hops, and loped toward the horse, picking up speed as she went. Jumping into the air, she came down hard with both feet on the high end of the springboard. The board popped down and up again, flinging her toward the horse. As she sailed over, she tucked her legs up under her and briefly pushed against the top of the horse with her extended hands, giving herself extra speed. She flew up and away from the horse, then straightened her body and landed on her feet. Immediately, she lifted both arms and stretched toward the ceiling. Then she turned and bowed slightly to Eric before marching from the thick landing pad.

"Good vault," Eric told her with an approving grin. To the other girls, he said, "It will be a while before you do one of those vaults. All you're to do today is run and jump onto the springboard, jump up on the top of the horse, then down on the other side. I'll spot you in case you start to fall."

He stationed himself at the edge of the thick mat behind the horse while the girls lined up at the end of the runway. Kim and Marcy moved back until they were at the end of the line. Kim watched as each girl trotted down the runway and tried to get up onto the horse. Some managed to land on top and jump down, but others didn't hit the springboard hard enough and just fell forward against the horse. Even Jay Jay didn't make it to the top.

Then it was Kim's turn. She felt her pulse begin to race. When she looked toward the horse, she thought she saw a face appear on one end, an evil face with wild red eyes. When she started to run, the horse grew bigger as it had in her dream. She hit the springboard and took off into the air. She did manage to land on top but toppled forward headlong toward the mat on the other side. Suddenly two strong hands reached out and grabbed her in midair.

"You gotta land on your feet, not your head," Eric said with a grin as he lifted her down to the mat. To the others he called, "You see, class? That's why you need a spotter. Safety is the key word in this gym. I don't want any of my girls getting hurt."

*My girls.*

That's what he had said. He might think her a troublemaker, but he had spotted her to save her from harm.

"Thank you," she said as she left the mat.

He nodded, smiled at her, and called, "Next!"

Marcy took her place at the end of the long mat. She stood for a moment staring with narrowed eyes toward the horse as though she were concentrating hard. She lifted her head and and straightened her shoulders. Then she gave a little hop, as Tish had done, and came pelting down the runway. Her thighs jiggled, her body bounced under the black leotard. When she pounced onto the springboard, it exploded with a loud pop, flinging her back into the air. She tucked her legs up under her and reached for the horse, touching it briefly with her hands, but instead of landing on top, she sailed right on over and landed on her feet on the other side. She straightened at once, as Tish had done, and lifted her arms toward the ceiling.

"Wow!" exclaimed Tish, clapping her hands.

Eric clapped, too. To Tish he said, "We may have ourselves a real vaulter here!"

Marcy flushed as bright a pink as the stripes on Kim's leotard. She hurried over to Kim, who whispered in wonder, "How did you ever do it?"

"Beats me. I thought I was headed for the moon."

"Bars next," Eric called.

Kim slid her eyes toward Lisa. The dark-haired girl stood alone to one side, again staring toward the bars with a strange expression. On impulse, Kim walked over to her.

"Don't worry," she murmured softly. "If you fall, he'll spot you the way he did me."

Lisa turned, looking at Kim from eyes which seemed bigger and darker than they really were because of the dark circles underneath. Kim decided she'd never seen such sad eyes.

"I . . . I don't think I can do it," Lisa whispered.

"Sure you can. Come on, you can stand with my friend and me."

Had she really said that? What would Marcy think? Nervously Kim led the way over to where Marcy was waiting. Marcy lifted her eyebrows at Kim as though to ask, What's this all about?

Kim shook her head to show she'd explain later. Aloud she said, "Lisa's a little scared of the bars, so I told her she could stand with us."

Marcy turned coolly toward Lisa, and Kim's heart sank with dread.

But Lisa didn't seem to notice Marcy's attitude as she exclaimed, "That vault you did—you're really good!"

With relief, Kim watched Marcy's coldness melt away.

"Do you really think so? I keep wondering if I will ever be able to do it again."

"All right, girls, watch Tish," Eric called.

Tish walked up behind the low bar, grabbed hold, lifted herself up, then kicked her legs forward and swung around under the bar and back up over the top so that she came to rest with her stomach against the top of the bar, her back slightly arched, her muscles tight.

"That's a back pullover," Eric explained.

"Piece of cake," Kim whispered to the others.

Sure enough, when her turn came, she was able to pull herself up and over the bar with no problem. She thought she deserved a pat from Eric, but all he did was nod at her and then call, "Okay, Marcy, you're next."

Marcy had to try three times before she could pull herself up onto the bar. Kim could tell that being overweight was not good for a gymnast on bars.

Then it was Lisa's turn. All the color left her face as she stepped forward and looked up at the bars. She started to lift herself up twice, but kept falling back, as though all the strength had left her arms. She flicked a desperate glance toward Kim.

Nodding her encouragement, Kim mouthed, "You can do it!"

Lisa took a deep breath. That time she managed to make it to the top of the bar, but when she looked down, she seemed to lose her strength. Her body bent double and she hung there over the bar like a wet sock. Eric grabbed her and lifted her away to set her on her feet.

"Trying to make up your own moves?" he joked.

Lisa nodded weakly. When she started to walk away, she stumbled over the guy wires beside the bars, and Eric had to catch her again.

42

Marcy flashed a quick glance toward Kim, asking silently, What is it with this person?

And again Kim tried to tell Marcy with her eyes that she'd explain later.

When they moved to the beam area, Eric pointed toward the beam that was four feet off the ground.

"High beam."

He pointed toward three other beams off to one side, each only about six inches off the floor.

"Low beams. You can practice walking on the low beams without a spotter, but stay off this high beam unless I'm there to catch you. Right now, though, I want each of you to jump up on the high beam just to see how it feels."

This time Kim went first. Although the beam was a full four inches wide, it seemed to shrink beneath her feet to a sliver. As she teetered there, she thought the floor looked a mile away. Nevertheless, she managed to take several wobbly steps before jumping off.

At the end of the class, Eric had one more thing to say. "Okay, class, a good gymnast has to be lean and mean. That means no junk food. No candy, no cupcakes, no greasy potato chips, no sodas. Three well-balanced meals a day, that's what I'm talking, with no snacks in between other than a piece of fruit, or a raw carrot, or celery. You got that?"

All the girls groaned. Kim glanced at Marcy and saw her roll her eyes toward the ceiling. Eric laughed at their reactions.

"I know it's hard, but eating right gives you a stronger body. Jog every day, and do your stretching exercises.

**43**

And if you want a doughnut . . . well, eat an apple, instead.''

"I *love* doughnuts, I *hate* apples," Marcy muttered to Kim from the corner of her mouth.

"Okay, class dismissed."

When Eric said that, the girls burst into noisy chatter and ran to the clothing baskets. While Kim and Marcy got into their shorts and shirts, Lisa pulled a pair of white shorts over her green leotard.

Again acting on impulse, Kim said to Lisa, "Would you like to come home with us and have a cookie?"

"You mean apple," Marcy murmured.

But the shadowed look had returned to Lisa's face. "I—I have to get right home. My mom needs me."

"Did you ride here on your bike?"

"No, I walked."

"Well, we're on our bikes," Kim said, "but we could ride them along beside you and see where you live—"

"No!" Lisa shouted the word so rudely that Kim flinched with shock. "No. We're busy today. Some other time, okay?"

"Sure, okay," Kim replied.

But it wasn't okay. Kim had thought she could be friends with Lisa. Now she felt slapped down, and she could tell Marcy felt that way, too.

"Come on, Kim, let's get out of here," Marcy growled, grabbing her arm.

For a moment, Kim thought she saw the glisten of tears in Lisa's eyes, but the girl blinked quickly and then set her mouth in a firm line. She grabbed her shoulder bag and hurried out the door, not looking back.

**44**

"See, I told you she was stuck-up," Marcy hissed.

Kim slowly shook her head.

"She acts like she's hiding something, like she has a secret." She began to grin. "Hey, let's follow her! But we mustn't let her see us."

Marcy's eyes lighted with excitement. "Okay, let's go!"

# Chapter 6

When they got outside they saw Lisa already headed down the sidewalk.

"Better leave our bikes locked up here," Kim suggested. "We can stay out of sight easier if we're on foot."

They slipped from yard to yard, hiding behind bushes and trees. Getting across the streets between blocks proved to be the hardest, for that's when they were the most exposed. They had to wait until there was no traffic coming, then dart across the street fast and hope they could reach a hiding spot before Lisa looked back. Once they had just dropped down behind a hedge when Lisa glanced over her shoulder.

"Whew, that was close!" Kim muttered, feeling a flutter of fear in her stomach.

They traveled through three blocks with houses, then entered a block where there were several small stores. Kim and Marcy ducked into a hardware store and watched through the plate glass window as Lisa crossed the street to a service station and entered the rest room there.

After a few minutes she emerged with her hiking bag slung over her shoulder. She was now wearing a pink sundress.

"She's taken off her leotard!" Marcy exclaimed.

"Weird," said Kim. "Why didn't she wait until she got home?"

"Don't ask me. Come on, let's not lose her."

The girls left the hardware store and followed Lisa down a side street lined with older houses where the trees were thick and tall, the bushes shaggy. Tracking here was easier, for there were plenty of places to hide.

They crossed the street to the next block where the houses looked even older. The third house down was over two stories tall with little attic windows peeking out from beneath high-pitched eaves. There was a round tower on one corner, like the tower of a castle, and it had a steep cone-shaped roof with a weathervane on top shaped like a Halloween cat.

Kim and Marcy dropped down behind a lilac bush and peered through a hole in the branches.

"What a strange house!" Kim muttered. "Maybe a witch lives there."

To her surprise, Lisa left the sidewalk and climbed the steps to the front porch. She paused a moment before the door, her shoulders drooping. After a moment, she pulled open the front door and disappeared inside.

"Good grief, is *that* where she lives?" exclaimed Marcy.

The two girls looked at each other.

"Did you see how she didn't want to go in?" Kim said. "Marcy, I think she really is in trouble. Maybe her

**48**

father beats her or something. Maybe he drinks. Or maybe that really is a witch's house, and she's under an evil spell."

"Oh, Kim, get serious!"

Marcy gave Kim a shove which caught her off-balance and sent her sprawling out into the grass beside the bush. As Kim stood up, she looked again toward the house and froze with shock.

There was a face in the upstairs tower window. A strange face with long dark hair. A woman dressed in black—

"The witch!" Kim yelled, her pulse pounding in her throat. "Run!"

She fled down the sidewalk. Through the roaring in her ears she heard footsteps pounding behind her. The witch—it was after her. She doubled her speed.

"Kim, wait up!"

"Run, Marcy, run!"

"Please, Kim . . ."

"Run!"

She dashed across the street into the next block. The footsteps still pounded behind her. She was afraid to look back.

Up ahead she saw the service station. There would be help there, other people. . . .

When she reached the station at last, she collapsed, gasping, beside one of the pumps. She took a chance on looking back down the block. The witch was not in sight, but Marcy was, staggering toward Kim with perspiration dripping from her chin.

"Wh-what is it? Why are we running?" Marcy asked.

"Didn't you see it? A face. There was a face in the tower window! A witch!"

Marcy gave Kim an incredulous look. "A what?"

The station attendant came striding up with a look of concern on his face. "What's the matter, is someone chasing you? Are you girls okay?"

Marcy shook her head. "We're fine, thank you. We-we're just out jogging."

She gave Kim a hard look as though to say, Don't mention the witch.

The man began to grin. "You're not supposed to run that hard when you jog. Better take it a little easier, okay?"

"Okay, thanks," Marcy said, keeping her voice casual. As soon as he was gone, she turned on Kim. "A witch? You're crazy."

Suddenly Kim knew that Marcy was right. Of course there was no witch in the house. Burning with embarrassment, she stood up and headed for the gym, followed by Marcy.

"How could I have been so stupid?"

"Don't feel bad, that place gave me the creeps, too." Marcy began to giggle. "But you sure scared me to death when you yelled 'Run!' I thought we'd had it."

Kim shuddered, remembering the woman in the window. She'd been pale, with shadowed eyes, and her black blouse had blended in with her long dark hair.

No wonder I thought she was a witch, Kim thought.

But who was she, and what did she have to do with Lisa? For Lisa was really frightened, Kim knew that for sure. Maybe she was in serious trouble. Maybe Kim and

Marcy were the only ones who could help. If they continued playing detective, perhaps they could find out what was going on.

She just hoped no one got hurt.

# Chapter 7

The next morning, Kim washed the breakfast dishes, then stepped out onto the patio and looked toward Marcy's house. She saw a red handkerchief taped to Marcy's bedroom window, their secret signal which meant, *Meet me in the clubhouse*.

After checking to make sure no one was watching, Kim hurried across the alley to the lilac bushes at the edge of Marcy's yard. She crawled through the tunnel and slipped through the sagging door into the shed.

"It's about time," Marcy grumbled. "I hung the signal over fifteen minutes ago."

Once Kim's eyes had adjusted to the dim light, she saw Marcy sitting at the table munching on a chocolate doughnut. On the table in front of Marcy sat a doughnut box which looked big enough to have held a dozen. Now the box was empty. Kim put her fists on her hips while looking at her friend accusingly.

Marcy shrugged, a guilty look on her face. "I can't help it. I love chocolate."

Quickly she popped the rest of the doughnut into her

53

mouth as though she was afraid Kim might take it away from her. Kim sat down at the table, shaking her head in disgust.

"I know you didn't call me over here to watch you eat. What's up?"

"Jogging," Marcy mumbled. She swallowed, clearing her mouth. "It'd be easier if we did it together. What do you say?"

"Okay by me. But how far do you have to jog to work off a dozen doughnuts?"

"Three doughnuts—that's all Mom had left. Chocolate's my favorite."

"I can tell."

"Look, don't give me a hard time! You're skinny, you can eat anything you please. It's not fair."

Kim thought about what Eric had said the day before. He'd included them all, fat and thin, when he'd said to cut out junk food. She didn't understand that. If you could eat anything and still stay slim, what did it matter?

"Anyway, are we going to jog or not?" Marcy asked sulkily.

Kim shrugged. "Sure, why not?"

After telling their mothers what they were going to do, the two girls set out. They loped in the direction of the gym, then turned down a side street where there was a large vacant lot. Kim jarred to a halt.

"Look!" she said, pointing.

In the middle of the lot walked Lisa with her back to them. She was pulling a red wagon which contained two lumpy garbage bags. Suddenly she stopped and leaned over to pick up something. She turned halfway around, examining the thing in her hand. It looked like an empty soda can. She dropped it back to the ground, lifted one foot, and brought her shoe smashing down. Kim heard a faint crunch as the can collapsed. Lisa picked up the flattened can and dropped it into one of the bags.

"Why's she doing that?" Marcy whispered.

"I don't know."

Lisa turned, then froze in her tracks, staring in their direction.

"Just act normal," Kim muttered from the corner of her mouth to Marcy. She plastered a bright smile on her face. "Hi!"

Lisa watched them approach without replying. Her face was tight, her eyes wary.

"We were just out jogging," Kim explained. She glanced toward the bulging garbage bags. "You collecting cans?"

"What of it?" Lisa demanded.

"Hey, no big deal. Just asking." Again Kim noticed the dark circles under the girl's eyes. "Recycling cans . . . that's a good thing to do."

Some of the wariness left Lisa's face. "Do you do that, too?"

"Well, no, but I saw a show about it on TV. You can get money for old aluminum cans."

*Money.*

Kim thought of the old house where Lisa lived. Maybe Lisa's family was poor. Maybe she had to gather cans to help pay the bills.

"There's one," Marcy cried. She darted toward a clump of weeds and dug out a battered can which she carried back to Lisa.

55

"You have to smash them flat, like this," Lisa said. She stamped down on the can as she had before.

Kim saw a can lying near an old board. "There's another one." She retrieved it and smashed it as Lisa had taught her, then dropped the can into the sack. "People sure are trashy, aren't they, throwing their junk around. Have you gathered this whole wagonload this morning?"

Lisa nodded. "I've been collecting cans ever since I moved here. There's a recycling center over on Oak Street, about five blocks away."

Kim nodded. She'd driven past it many times with her folks.

"They—well, they actually pay you for cans," Lisa went on.

Kim turned her face away, afraid her expression would betray how sorry she felt for Lisa.

"I've got an idea!" Marcy put in brightly. "Let's run a race to see who can find the most cans on this lot. It'll be fun, like hunting Easter eggs."

Kim swung back, smiling once more at the idea of helping Lisa. "Sure, let's do that."

Lisa looked uncertainly back and forth between the two of them. "Well, if—if you really want to."

"One for the money, two for the show, three to get ready, and four to GO!" Marcy called.

Kim dashed off toward the far corner of the lot where she could see three cans winking beside a pile of rubble. While picking those up, she spotted a fourth one. Then, in some weeds next to a fence, she found two more cans. They were awkward to carry. When she tucked a couple of them under her arm, the sticky syrup dribbled

56

onto her blouse. She raced back and dumped the cans in a pile beside the wagon.

"These are mine, piled here in front!" she called.

"Okay," the girls shouted back.

Kim scurried off again. She found two more cans under a pile of rusting wire. She looked around but saw no more. When she raced back to the wagon, the other girls were already there.

"I found four," Lisa said.

"I found seven," Marcy put in.

Kim counted hers, then grinned. "Got you beat, I found eight."

They flattened the cans and stuffed them into the garbage bags. With difficulty, Lisa tied the tops of the bags shut.

"Got a full load," she said. "Guess I'd better head on over to the center."

"Can we come along?" Kim asked.

Lisa gave them both a tentative smile. "That'd be great. When it's full, the wagon's hard to pull."

That proved to be an understatement. While Lisa pulled, Kim pushed. Marcy walked alongside to steady the bulging sacks. Even so, they almost tipped over several times as they maneuvered up and down the curbs.

"How did you ever manage alone?" Kim finally gasped.

Lisa shook her head. "Not so well. I spilled a whole sack of cans in the gutter the other day."

Finally they reached the recycling center. The large fenced lot filled most of the block. There was a metal office building to one side with scales out in front. In another area, several men lifted stacks of newspaper onto a conveyor belt which fed into a noisy shredding machine. A forklift trundled by loaded with more papers. Bins filled with flattened cans sat in another spot, while loose paper plastered the high chain link fence. As the girls pulled the wagon into the yard, Kim wrinkled her nose at the dusty smell in the air.

A tall man in tan pants and shirt came out of the office to greet them. "Hi, Lisa! I see you got yourself some help today."

"Hello, Mr. Lewis. Yes, these are my friends, Kim and Marcy."

Kim smiled when Lisa called her a friend.

Lisa pulled the wagon toward the scales. She started to lift out one of the sacks, but Mr. Lewis strode forward, saying, "Here, I'll do that for you."

When he had weighed the cans, he jotted the numbers in a notebook he had in his pocket. He went into his office and soon returned carrying money and a receipt which he gave to Lisa. She picked up an old purse from the bottom of the wagon and started to drop in the money, then paused.

"You helped me," she said to Kim and Marcy. "I should share this with you."

The two girls shook their heads.

"Hey, it was fun!" Marcy exclaimed.

"Right," Kim echoed.

As the girls were leaving, Mr. Lewis called out, "Keep up the good work, Lisa!"

While they headed away, Kim decided to pretend she thought Lisa was only doing this to help clean up the city.

"Mr. Lewis is right, it's nice to keep the trash picked up," she said. "You're a good person."

To her surprise, Lisa sat down in the wagon and burst into tears. "No, I'm not. I'm awful!"

"What do you mean?" Marcy asked.

"I—I can't tell you." Lisa covered her face with her hands.

Kim knelt beside her and touched her arm. "Sure you can. We're your friends."

Lisa still kept her face covered. "It's—it's my mom. If she finds out. . . ."

"Finds out what?" Kim asked. But a terrible answer to that question had already popped into her mind. What if Lisa had stolen some money and was trying to get enough to pay it back?

"Finds out—finds out that I'm taking gymnastics," Lisa gulped.

Kim was so relieved she almost laughed. "She doesn't know? Why should she mind?"

Lisa lowered her hands, revealing a tear-streaked face. "You don't understand. It's because of my dad. *He's* the one who wanted me to take gymnastics, not Mom. He was—he was great. He could do anything."

*Was.* Lisa had said *was.*

Kim glanced toward Marcy and saw she'd caught it, too.

"My dad won ribbons all the time, and trophies," Lisa went on.

"Doing what?"

"Skiing, car racing. I told you, he could do anything."

Kim began to have a bad feeling. "Lisa, did your dad get hurt?"

59

Lisa took a shuddering breath. "He—he got killed. Skydiving. Three months ago, out in California, before we moved here."

Kim felt shock jolt through her whole body.

"Mom was there when it happened," Lisa continued. "She saw him fall. I'd gone to the movies, so I wasn't there."

Tears poured once more from her eyes and coursed down her cheeks. Kim couldn't stand it. She moved closer and put her arms around Lisa, trying to comfort her. Marcy joined them.

"We used to watch sports together on TV, Dad and me," Lisa said. "This spring we watched a rerun of girls doing gymnastics at the last Olympics, and Dad said he thought I'd be good at that. He told me he wanted me to start gymnastics as soon as school was out, and I promised him I would. But two weeks later . . ." She took a deep breath. "Two weeks later he died."

"Lisa, I'm so sorry." Kim held her close, wanting to ease her pain. Finally Lisa quieted, and the other two girls pulled away, still watching her anxiously. Lisa got a tissue from the purse and blew her nose.

"What's this business of your mom not knowing you're taking gymnastics?" Marcy asked.

Lisa's face twisted with misery. "Something . . . something's wrong with Mom now. Ever since we moved here to live with my grandmother, all Mom does is sit in her room and stare out the window. She won't let me swim, she won't let me ride my skateboard. I guess . . . well, I guess she's afraid something will happen to me, too."

"But you promised your Dad . . ." Kim began.

"That's right," Lisa interrupted. "I *promised* him I'd take gymnastics this summer, my last promise to him."

Suddenly Kim had the whole picture. "But you can't tell your mother about it because she'd worry. You have to earn the money for the class yourself."

Kim nodded. "My dad, I told you, he could do anything. He used to be a champion wind surfer, too. But me, I can't do anything. I'm a nobody."

Kim shared a long look with Marcy. When Marcy nodded, Kim stepped forward and took both of Lisa's hands.

"Welcome to the club."

# Chapter 8

The girls initiated Lisa into the club that very day. They started with the Blood Oath.

Kim did not like having the end of her finger pricked, but every story she'd ever read about secret clubs had said that a blood oath was necessary, so she and Marcy had written the oath into their original rules.

Now Marcy swabbed the end of Kim's finger with Kleenex dipped in rubbing alcohol. She then dipped a needle into the alcohol. Kim shuddered. To her, the needle looked as big as a pencil.

"Here goes," said Marcy, holding the needle above the end of Kim's finger. "You ready?"

Kim wasn't, but she nodded yes. There was a sharp prick as Marcy jabbed the needle into the skin. Blood welled up at once in a bright red drop.

"Did it hurt?" Lisa asked anxiously.

Kim blinked back tears. "Just for a second."

Quickly Marcy jabbed her own finger and then Lisa's. The three girls touched their fingers together, mingling their blood.

"Repeat after me," Kim said to Lisa in a solemn tone. "I, Lisa Andrelli—"

"I, Lisa Andrelli—"

"Do hereby swear—"

"Do hereby swear—"

"To be loyal to the Nobody Club and all it's members, to obey the club rules, and to keep its secrets, even under pain of torture and death."

When Lisa had finished the oath, Kim showed Lisa how to make the secret sign. "Like this, with your three middle fingers together and your thumb and little finger spread apart."

"If you're careful, no one else but us will know what you're doing," said Marcy. "Watch."

She leaned against the wall and rested one hand on her hip with the three middle fingers pointing toward her stomach and the thumb and little finger spread out.

"Or like this," Kim said.

She casually placed a hand on top of the table with her fingers arranged in the sign.

"Hey, that's good!" Lisa exclaimed. "I wouldn't know what you were doing if you hadn't told me."

Lisa sighed and stretched as though she were getting bored. She covered her yawn with a hand arranged in the secret sign.

Kim laughed with delight. "You catch on fast!"

"Let's say you got in trouble at school," put in Marcy. "We'd make the sign to say, 'Don't forget, you have a friend."

Lisa's eyes filled with tears. "When I moved here . . . well, coming into a new school two weeks before it's over, that's really hard. Everybody has their own friends

64

and they don't talk to someone new. I used to watch the two of you. You looked so close. I wanted to say hi, but, well, I was afraid, I thought you'd snub me or something. I thought you were both really stuck-up.''

"We thought *you* were stuck-up," Kim admitted sheepishly.

"But that's over," Marcy put in quickly. "You're one of us now."

Kim took it up. "Tell you what. Let's jog together every day, taking a different street each time. We'll carry garbage bags and collect cans on the way back. Or . . ." She paused, letting the idea grow in her mind. "Or how about this? We could go around and ask all the neighbors to save their cans for us. Newspapers, too. What do you think?"

"We could make handouts to leave at the doors where the people aren't home," Marcy suggested.

"That's a good idea."

The three girls sat down at the table, interrupting each other eagerly as the plan grew.

"If we each take ten houses—"

"That's one newspaper per house per day. That's . . ." Kim did some quick figuring in her head. "That's seventy papers apiece per week!"

"Which is . . ." Marcy wrote on the table with her finger, her tongue sticking out. ". . . which is two hundred and eighty papers apiece per month, which is . . ."

She paused, her face screwed up.

"That's over eight hundred papers a month!" Lisa suddenly exclaimed.

"Wow!"

They all stared at each other in amazement.

"That's an awful lot of papers," Marcy said seriously. "We can't carry all those to the recycling center in Lisa's wagon. And we'll have to store them somewhere during the month."

"How about the clubhouse?" Kim asked.

"Well . . ."

"Scott. Maybe Scott would drive us to the center in Dad's station wagon." To Lisa she added, "Scott's my big brother."

"Humph! You know Scott," Marcy said to Kim in a sarcastic voice. "If we got to him, he'll ask 'What's in it for me?' "

"Let's give it a try."

They hurried to Kim's house where they found Scott lying on his bed listening to a rock tape. Kim explained they'd decided to collect old cans and papers, and asked Scott if he'd drive them to the center once a month. He chewed his lip, giving her a crafty look.

"What's in it for me?" he demanded.

"Told you so!" cried Marcy.

"Shut up, fatso." Scott slid off his bed and stood up. He was tall and lanky, wearing jeans and a white T-shirt with a picture of Superman and the words SUPER SCOTT. His blond hair fell in an unruly cowlick over his gray-green eyes. Right now those eyes surveyed the girls with greed.

"Well, I'll carry the garbage out for you on trash day," Kim volunteered.

"Not enough. What else?"

Kim glanced around his room and gulped. His bed was unmade. Dirty clothes lay scattered everywhere. A

66

black banana peel hung over one side of his wastebasket like a dead eel.

"Um, I'll clean your room for you, too."

"Every week," he said, looking at her with narrowed eyes.

"Now wait a minute! You only have to drive us once a month, so I only have to clean your room once a month, okay?"

Slowly he grinned. He reached out and ruffled her hair which she knew he knew she hated. "Okay, spaghetti legs, it's a deal."

Having gotten that settled, the girls retired to Kim's room to letter their handouts. Kim found thirty sheets of paper, plus pens and crayons. After deciding on the wording, each girl lettered and decorated ten pages. Kim outlined her pages with a red, white and blue border. Marcy drew a soda pop can with a smiling face on each of her pages. But Lisa proved to be the most artistic, drawing funny little stick figures carrying cans and newspapers across the bottom of each page.

The handbills read:

---

RECYCLING PROJECT!
SAVE YOUR NEWSPAPERS AND
ALUMINUM CANS FOR US!
WE'LL PICK THEM UP ONCE A WEEK.
THANK YOU.
THREE NEIGHBORHOOD COLLECTORS!!!!!

---

"Because," Kim explained, "T-N-C will stand for The Nobody Club, but no one will guess."

In smaller print below the message they included their names and phone numbers.

When they had finished, they showed the handouts to Kim's mother.

"What a good summer project!" Mrs. Turner exclaimed.

Kim felt relieved. She'd wondered what they would do if her mother did not approve.

"Just one thing," her mother went on. "You must never go around door-to-door alone. All three of you must be together, because—"

"—because there are sometimes bad people in this world who can hurt you," Kim interrupted in a bored voice. She'd heard that lecture before.

"Don't be impertinent," said her mother sternly. "Just be careful, that's all." Then, smiling again, she asked, "Where are you going to store all these cans and papers?"

The three girls looked nervously at each other. They did not want to explain about the secret clubhouse.

Mrs. Turner chuckled. "You didn't think about that, did you? Look, Kim, I'm sure your father won't care if you use one corner of our garage. Will that be okay?"

"Thanks, Mom," Kim said, breaking into a big grin.

"Now," Mrs. Turner went on, "how about some lunch?"

"Sounds good to me," said Marcy.

"I'll have to call my grandmother first," Lisa said, some of the joy leaving her face. "My mom . . . well, she'll begin to worry, you know."

When she hung up the receiver, she announced happily, "Grandma says it's okay, I can stay!"

After lunch, the girls distributed their handbills.

"I like to see young people doing these nice things," beamed an older woman when they had explained their project. "My name's Mrs. Colbert, and you can count on my help."

When the girls were walking away, she called after them, "God bless!"

When all the handbills were gone, Lisa said, "I'd better get home now before Mom gets upset."

Kim and Marcy walked with her to Kim's front yard where Lisa had left her wagon. They said goodbye and Lisa started down the sidewalk, pulling the wagon behind her. Suddenly she stopped and looked back, her eyes shining. She lifted one hand and brushed the hair back from her eyes, using the secret sign. In return Kim casually rubbed her chin with her three middle fingers while Marcy hooked her fingers around her hips.

After Lisa had gone beyond hearing, Marcy sighed. "That poor kid. She's really got it rough."

Kim nodded. Worry grew inside her mind like an ugly patch of weeds. She thought of that strange pale face framed in the tower window. What if the club didn't earn enough money for Lisa to stay in class? What if Lisa's mother found out about the gymnastics class? What if she said Lisa had to quit?

She shook her head, trying to get rid of all those "what ifs," but they would not go away.

"What if we can't help her?" Marcy asked, echoing Kim's fears.

Kim straightened her shoulders. "We can do it. We're—"

"We're Nobodies," Marcy reminded her.

"Well, the Nobodies are just gonna have to become Somebodies!"

Marcy grinned and snapped to attention, saluting Kim with their three-finger sign. "Right! We can do it." She wavered. "Can't we?"

"Sure we can," Kim said, trying to sound positive. She hoped it was true.

# Chapter 9

On the day of the next gymnastics class, Kim and Marcy arrived at the gym ahead of Lisa. Kim was beginning to fear that something must have happened to keep Lisa at home when the door opened and the dark-haired girl dashed in. Kim and Marcy ran over to her.

"Is anything wrong?" Kim asked anxiously.

Lisa grimaced. "Grandma kept giving me chores to do for her this morning. I didn't think I'd ever get away."

"What did you finally tell her?"

"That I was meeting my two new friends. That's the truth, anyway. She says she's glad I have friends now."

"We *are* your friends. We'll help you all we can," Kim said. She and Marcy both gave Lisa a quick hug.

Just then Jay Jay walked by.

"What's this, the Three Musketeers?" she asked sarcastically.

"That's right," Kim replied coolly. "We're going to become the best gymnasts this place has ever seen."

"That'll be the day."

After Jay Jay had walked off with her nose in the air, Marcy muttered, "She makes me sick."

During class Eric suggested that the girls should begin doing chin-ups at home every day to strengthen their arms for the bars.

"Maybe you could use a swing set," he suggested.

While the three girls were getting dressed after class, Marcy said, "Joanie's got a swing set. Why don't both of you come to my backyard this afternoon and we'll try it?"

"I'll come if I can get away again," Lisa promised.

She called Kim during lunch to say she'd be there. Kim waited until Lisa showed up, then the two girls walked over to Marcy's backyard together. Marcy was already waiting for them.

"Look, I've built a gym! See, here are the bars." She pointed toward the swing set. "And here is a low beam." She gestured toward a long narrow board lying in the grass. "There's the horse." She extended one finger toward an old clothes hamper with a padded top. "And there is the floor mat." She indicated the grassy lawn.

Kim and Lisa both laughed.

"Great!" Kim said. "Where do we start?"

Marcy paced back and forth, imitating Eric's walk. "Since this is my yard, I get to be the coach. Stretching exercises first."

She unfolded a blanket and spread it on the grass. Sitting like Tish in front of the other girls, she counted aloud as she led them through their exercises.

"You warmed up now?" she said. "Okay, let's try chin-ups. Me first."

She climbed up on a swing and reached to one side to grab hold of the top bar. She swung into space and hung there for a moment before trying to pull up.

"Ugh!"

"Try again."

"Uh . . . oh . . . ooh." Grunting with effort, Marcy managed to lift herself about three inches each time. Finally she dropped to the ground and held out her hands, showing how red her palms were from the pressure. "That's hard!"

Lisa went next. She didn't seem to be as afraid as she had the first day at the gym. She managed to chin herself four times before letting go.

Then it was Kim's turn. She grabbed the bar and kicked away from the swing. Her body stretched toward the ground, hanging heavily from her tightly gripped hands. The first time she tried to lift herself up, she rose only about six inches. She got a little farther the second time. After three more tries, she managed to lift all the way for one chin-up. Then she, too, dropped to the ground.

"You're right, that's not easy."

Next they practiced walking back and forth on the narrow board, pretending it was the beam. Kim found she could keep her balance with no problem. She even tried the hitch kick that Tish had taught them. Kicking her right leg high in the air, she then kicked with her left leg as the right leg came down. She landed on her right foot with her left foot forward.

If I can do it here, why can't I do it at the gym? she asked herself.

But she already knew the answer. Here, the board

rested right on the ground, so she wasn't afraid of falling off. That high beam at the gym felt as though it was about a hundred feet in the air.

Just then the back door to Marcy's house opened and Joanne came out onto the steps. She was wearing a blue-and-white-checked sunsuit. Her ruined hair looked even worse than Kim had remembered.

Lisa let out a gasp. "What happened to her?"

Marcy rolled her eyes toward heaven. "Don't ask."

Joanne climbed carefully down the steps and came smiling toward the girls. "Hi!"

"Hi yourself," Lisa responded.

Joanne's smile widened. "Cut haiah!"

Kim got down on her knees and looked Joanne in the eye. "Don't cut any more hair! You hear me? Don't cut hair!"

The little girl began shaking her head. "Don't cut haiah?"

*"Don't cut hair,"* replied Kim emphatically. "Now remember that."

Lisa stared down at the little girl. "She's pretty if you don't look at the bald spot. Couldn't you put a wig on her until her hair grows out?"

Kim considered it. "Do they make wigs for kids?"

"You have a wig, Kim," Marcy reminded her. "The one your mom gave you for dress-up, remember?"

"But that was Mom's. It's awful big." Kim looked once more at Joanne. "Let's try it anyway."

Marcy raced up the steps. "Hey, Mom," she yelled, "I'm taking Joanie over to Kim's!"

"Okay" came a voice through the kitchen door.

They hurried across the alley, into Kim's house, and

**74**

down the hallway to her room. Kim went to her bureau and opened the bottom drawer where she kept her dress-up clothes, although she and Marcy hadn't played dress-up for a long time. She rummaged through her collection of old dresses, beads, hats, and shoes before she found the wig wadded up in a corner. She pulled it out and shook it, fluffing the brown curls.

"Here, Joanie, try this on."

Joanne marched over and took the wig. She draped it across the top of her head and smiled up at Kim.

The girls laughed.

"No, Joanie, like this."

Kim took the wig and stretched the elastic lining to slip the hair down over the little girl's head. When Kim released the elastic, it snapped securely into place, surrounding Joanne's small face with a huge cloud of curls. She looked top-heavy, a funny little person with clown hair, like some cartoon character on a Saturday morning TV show.

Marcy giggled again. "I think we're just gonna have to wait for her real hair to grow out."

But when Marcy reached to take the wig off Joanne, the little girl grabbed it with both hands and hung on tight. "Mine!" she yelled, her face turning red. "I keep it!"

Marcy shrugged. "Guess we'd better let her wear it for a while. She'll get tired of it pretty soon."

Lisa dug an old evening gown out of the drawer. It was made of pink chiffon and had sequins around the neck. "This is pretty. Can I try it on?"

Kim had thought she was getting too old for dress-up, but now the idea seemed like fun.

"Sure, why not? What was that game we used to play, Marcy?"

"You were Princess Rainbow, imprisoned in a dungeon by—"

Kim took it up as the memory came back. "—by the Monster King. And you were Prince Trueheart, fighting your way through the Seven Deadly Trials to rescue me."

Laughing together over the story, they dug in the drawer for costumes.

"Since you've got on that pretty dress, you be Princess Rainbow this time," Kim said to Lisa, "and I can wear this Halloween monster mask and be the Monster King."

Marcy draped an old red curtain like a cape around her own shoulders. "Prince Trueheart," she announced, striking a pose.

"Me, me," cried Joanne.

Marcy grinned. "You can be the Magic Dwarf."

She pinned a blue towel around Joanne's shoulders to make another cape and poked the child's fat little feet into Kim's old majorette boots. Then she handed Joanne a twirling baton for a wand.

"There, how's that?"

Joanne nodded, a big smile on her face. She stomped across the floor in the boots. "I a magic dwaf!"

Kim searched through a box in one corner of her closet. "Where are all those props we made—the crowns, the swords . . . ?"

"I've got those over at my house, remember?" Marcy said. "Come on, we can finish dressing there."

They paraded back across the alley to Marcy's house.

**76**

"Hi, Mom, we're back!" Marcy yelled when they'd entered the kitchen.

"Okay." Mrs. Doyle's voice sounded muffled and far away, as though she might be in the bathroom.

Just then the doorbell rang.

"Will you get that?" called Mrs. Doyle.

Marcy looked down at herself, decked out in a belted blouse for a tunic with her jeans tucked into black rubber rain boots and the red cap hanging around her shoulders.

"Wouldn't you know it!" she remarked in dismay.

The doorbell rang again.

"Marcy!" her mother called in a louder voice.

"All right, I'm going!" Marcy called back. To the others she groaned, "I feel like such a fool."

"The least we can do is come with you," Kim said. "Then you won't look quite so stupid if it isn't just you alone."

They all trailed through the living room to the front door. They opened it to see a middle-aged man wearing a suit with a vest and a tie.

"Well, hello," he said, smiling down at the four of them. "My, aren't you cute?"

Marcy's face flamed as red as her cape. "May I help you?"

"Yes. I'm Lewis Dalton, owner of Dalton's Department Store, and I'd like to speak with your mother." His eyes sought, and then found, Joanne who was trying to hide behind Lisa.

"There you are, you little sweetheart! How's my Beautiful Child?"

Marcy exchanged a startled look with Kim. "Co-

77

come on in and sit down,'' she stammered, leading the way into the living room.

Still beaming, Mr. Dalton sat on the couch while the three older girls took chairs and stared back at him, not knowing what to say. Joanne leaned against Marcy's knee with her thumb in her mouth. She always sucked her thumb when she met a strange grown-up. Kim felt glad that Joanne had on the wig so Mr. Dalton could not see the bald spot on top of his Beautiful Child.

Mrs. Doyle came hurrying into the room. She slid to a halt and lifted her eyebrows at the sight of the girls in their strange outfits.

Mr. Dalton rose to his feet and held out his hand. ''Mrs. Doyle! How nice to see you again!''

She turned away from the girls and shook the man's hand. ''Hello, Mr. Dalton. What brings you here today?''

He nodded toward Joanne with a big smile. ''I just stopped by to say hello to my Beautiful Child.''

Joanne seemed to feel more secure with her mother in the room. Taking her thumb from her mouth, she stepped forward and announced proudly, ''I a magic dwaf!''

Mr. Dalton chuckled. ''Isn't she precious? Look, I'll come right to the point. My store is planning an advertising campaign for a new line of children's clothing, and we'd like to feature Joanne on the cover of our catalogue. I can just see it, all those pretty golden curls!''

Kim's stomach turned over. She wished she could sink through the floor and disappear.

Mrs. Doyle cleared her throat. ''I—uh . . .''

''We wouldn't work her too hard,'' the man hastened to explain. ''And you would come with her, of course,

**78**

so she'd feel at home. We wouldn't want our little sweetheart to get lonely."

He beamed at Joanne again. She took a few steps closer, holding up the baton.

"I a magic dwaf," she repeated.

"You're a little princess, that's what you are," he replied, "but why have you covered up your beautiful hair?"

He reached for the wig. Joanne stepped back out of his reach.

"Mine!" she said, starting to frown.

"Mr. Dalton . . ." Mrs. Doyle began, but he was not to be stopped.

"Just one little peek," he told Joanne. "Just one? I want to see how pretty you'll look in your picture."

He leaned forward and grabbed hold of the wig. As Joanne jerked away, the wig popped off in Mr. Dalton's hand.

"Argh!" screamed Joanne, her face an angry scarlet. Her chopped-off hair bristled above her forehead like a shaved broom.

Mr. Dalton stood frozen, his mouth open, his eyes bugging out. Wailing like a police car siren, Joanne swung the baton and whacked him hard across the knees. He let out a yell and bent double, dropping the wig to clutch his legs.

"Mine!" Joanne cried.

She dropped the baton and grabbed up the wig. She tugged it crookedly back over the top of her head, managing to cover one eye.

"Mine," she repeated.

This is the end, Kim thought. Marcy's mom is gonna kill us for sure.

Mr. Dalton straightened with a groan.

"I—I guess you won't be using Joanne for your cover girl," Mrs. Doyle said in a tight voice.

"No, I guess not."

He limped toward the front door, followed by Mrs. Doyle. Kim glanced over at the other two girls and saw them both slumped down in their chairs. Marcy's face was very pale.

Mrs. Doyle let Mr. Dalton out, then returned to the living room where she surveyed the girls with a grim expression. But as Kim watched, she saw Mrs. Doyle's face begin to change. First one corner of the woman's mouth twitched, then the other. She began to smile. The smile became a grin. She choked on a chuckle, then burst into laughter. All of a sudden she was laughing so hard that she collapsed on the couch.

"Did you—did you see his face?" she gasped. "When that wig came off his Beautiful Child . . . !"

Kim began to laugh, too, a little nervously at first. But the more she thought about it, the funnier it seemed. Her laughter grew until tears were pouring down her cheeks. She realized that the other girls were laughing, too.

Joanne giggled. Marching up to her mother, she said, "I a magic dwaf."

"You're an imp and should be spanked," Mrs. Doyle said sternly. But when she looked at the wig tilted over Joanne's eye, she once more began to laugh.

Wiping her eyes at last, she said, "This calls for a party. Let's go out in the kitchen and have ice cream and cake."

80

Kim saw a pained look cross Marcy's face. "Ah, Mom . . . could we have apples, instead?"

"Apples?" Mrs. Doyle fixed Marcy with an astonished look. "You don't like apples."

"It's gotta be apples."

"That's certainly a change!"

Later, as they munched apples in the kitchen, Kim looked toward Mrs. Doyle and asked, "Are you not mad at us anymore? About Joanne's hair, I mean?"

"I was plenty mad at first," Mrs. Doyle admitted, "but let's face it, her hair will grow out again. There are a lot worse things in this world than having a bald child." She suddenly sputtered with laughter again. "That poor man. I wish I'd had a camera."

Kim grinned in response. She was glad that Marcy's mom had regained her sense of humor. But Mr. Doyle— well, that was another story. And as for Lisa's mother . . .

The tragedy of Lisa's situation settled down over Kim like a gray fog.

Yes, she thought, there are worse things than ruined hair.

# Chapter 10

During the middle of the next class at the gym Kim pushed her hair back from her perspiring forehead and muttered to Marcy, "They oughta pay us to work this hard." She couldn't believe how many new skills they were learning on all the equipment.

"Okay, let me tell you some more about that meet this class will hold at the end of the summer," Eric said. "Tish has made up some routines for you to learn in each event. Later on, if you stay in gymnastics, you'll learn harder routines which have been made up at the national level for girls all over the country. Don't forget, we will have judges for this meet, and you'll be scored on how well you do."

The whole class groaned except for Jay Jay. She just smiled in a superior way.

"Okay, today we'll start learning the floor routine," he said. "It combines both tumbling and dancing. Once you know all the moves, you'll do it to music. Each kick, or turn, or leap, has to come on a particular beat of the music. Watch now, and Tish'll show you."

Eric started a tape machine which sat on a table near the floor mat. Looking slim and pretty in a blue leotard, Tish struck a dramatic pose in the middle of the floor mat. When the music started, she began dancing and tumbling around the floor. In one place she did a body wave, hunching in and contracting her stomach, then arching her backbone forward so smoothly that her whole body seemed to ripple from her feet up to the top of her head.

"Oh, my goodness," Marcy groaned in Kim's ear. "I can't ever pull my stomach in like that."

In another place Tish did a split leap, then a series of cartwheels, in another place a handstand followed by a forward roll. Toward the end of the routine she did a roundoff, which was a kind of special cartwheel that Eric had said was important to do right.

When Tish finished with another dramatic pose, Kim clapped her hands, as did the other girls, but underneath, she felt scared. There was no way she could ever learn all that. Beside her, she heard Marcy and Lisa moan.

"We're doomed," muttered Marcy.

Tish looked toward them and grinned. "We've got some nervous people here," she called to Eric. To the class, she said, "Don't worry, we'll learn it a pass at a time. A pass—that's one part of the whole pattern. You'll get it, you'll see."

Tish had the class count off and get into four lines.

Just my luck, Kim thought bleakly when she found herself first in her line. She glanced over her shoulder toward the girls behind her: Lisa, Marcy, and a short stocky blonde girl named Anne Everett.

"Trade places with me?" she whispered.

They all shook their heads.

Kim took a deep breath and stepped out onto the mat. Her pulse was racing, her mouth dry. She glanced from the corner of her eye toward the tall, lean, black girl next to her. She remembered, from roll call, that the girl's name was Laurie Jones. Beyond Laurie stood a brown-haired girl in a yellow leotard. Beth something, Kim couldn't remember her last name. The last girl on the mat, looking very confident, was Jay Jay.

Wouldn't you know it! Kim thought.

"All right, opening pose," Tish announced.

Feeling like a fool, Kim tried to copy the way Tish was standing. She lowered her eyes toward the floor so she wouldn't have to look at the other girls.

"No, Kim, chin up," commanded Tish. "Keep your head high. Look proud."

Kim felt her face burn as she tilted her chin. She felt silly, standing in that dumb pose with her nose pointed at the ceiling.

"Okay, step like this, and like this," said Tish, demonstrating. "Laurie, point your toes. Turn like this, arms up. Stretch, Beth, stretch! Now the body wave . . ."

When Kim bent and pulled her stomach in as tight as possible, then arched forward in a flowing motion the way Tish had, her vertebrae creaked in protest.

As they finished the first pass, Tish called out, "Okay, people, that wasn't too bad for the first time. Next group of girls, out on the mat."

Quickly Kim hurried to the back of her line. Anne Everett glanced toward her and grinned sympathetically. Kim rolled her eyes in reply, to show how awful it had been. Then she peered past Anne and Marcy to watch Lisa out on the floor. Kim thought Lisa looked graceful as she moved through the different steps; but when Lisa finished and ran to stand behind Kim, she, too, made a face.

Marcy was right—her body didn't wave, it jiggled like Jello. Kim heard a snort of laughter down the line and looked in time to see Jay Jay lift a hand to cover a grin. Marcy stumbled through the rest of the pass, looking miserable.

Anne Everett did well.

Then it was Kim's turn again. The second time through proved to be easier than the first.

After they'd all gone through the pass six times, Eric said, "Okay, now we'll do it to music."

To Kim the music sounded like a jumble of notes with no pattern. She couldn't figure out where to kick, where to turn.

That afternoon, trying to run through the moves again in her backyard with Marcy and Lisa, Kim asked, "Do you think we'll ever get it?"

Marcy shook her head glumly. "Not in a million years."

Scott came ambling out onto the patio. He was licking a chocolate ice cream cone and carrying a boombox, a big portable radio with double cassette player which the football team had awarded him after he'd made the winning touchdown in last year's homecoming game. Music blasted from the stereo speakers.

"You sure look stupid jumping around out here!" he yelled over the top of the music. "I wouldn't make a fool of myself like that on a bet."

As he sprawled onto a lawn chair, Kim cried, "Turn that off and go back in the house!"

"Why?"

"We were here first."

"It's a free country." He took another lick of ice cream.

"We can't practice with you out here."

"Why not?"

"Because."

He grinned. "Because I'll point at you and laugh a lot?" He took another lick of ice cream, a long, lingering lick.

Kim glanced toward Marcy. The plump girl's eyes were fixed on the chocolate cone.

Tossing her head in frustration, Kim advanced on Scott. "You make me so mad!"

He eyed her placidly. "What are brothers for?"

"Scott!"

He turned up the volume even higher, drowning her words. She clapped her hands over her ears.

"Turn that thing down!"

"Make me."

Kim darted forward and grabbed the radio out of his hand.

"Hey!" he yelled, jumping to his feet. As he lunged toward Kim, the ice cream flew out of his cone and splatted against the front of Marcy's shirt. The brown glob slid down her stomach and plopped into the grass.

"Now look what you've done!" Marcy cried, leaping forward to sock Scott on the arm.

Ignoring Marcy, Scott yelled at Kim, "If you break that, you'll pay for it!"

Kim took off at a run around the picnic table. Scott pounded after her. She dodged away, thrusting the radio into Lisa's hands. Scott tried to twist after her, but fell into the grass. His face landed right in the middle of the glob of ice cream. When he pushed himself to his knees, his mouth and chin were smeared with chocolate.

"Now who looks stupid?" Kim scoffed, pointing her finger at his dripping chin.

He wiped his arm across his mouth, smearing the chocolate even worse, and scrambled to his feet. "When I catch you—!"

Just then the patio doors slammed open and Mrs. Turner hurried from the house. "What's going on out here? I could hear you all the way into the living room."

"Scott's bothering us," Kim began.

"I am not," Scott interrupted angrily. "Make them give me back my radio."

"He's been making fun of us," Kim cried. "Tell him to leave us alone."

"Stop!" Mrs. Turner held up both hands in a commanding way.

Lisa turned off the music. In the sudden silence Mrs. Turner looked back and forth between Kim and Scott.

"How old are the two of you, anyway?" she asked sarcastically.

Kim always hated it when her mother used that tone of voice.

"I swear, you both act like you're in kindergarten," Mrs. Turner went on. "Kim, give Scott back his radio."

Kim took the radio from Lisa and handed it to her brother, who accepted it with a glare.

"Now, Scott, quit giving these girls a hard time," Mrs. Turner went on sternly.

Scott shrugged. "It's boring out here anyway. I guess I'll go see what's on TV."

He ambled past his mother and back into the house. She watched him go while shaking her head. "I don't know why the two of you can't get along better," she said to Kim.

"He started it."

"That's enough. I don't want to hear any more." Mrs. Turner sighed and walked back into the house.

Marcy looked down at her soiled clothes.

"You'd better go home and soak those in cold water before they stain," Lisa advised.

Marcy nodded. "Yeah, I guess so."

As she turned toward her own yard, she gave a backwards glance over her shoulder toward the brown puddle in the grass.

"What a waste," she sighed. "Chocolate's my favorite."

# Chapter 11

"Whew! This is a bigger job than I expected."

Kim collapsed in the empty wagon and fanned herself with her hand as she surveyed the pile of newspapers and cans stacked in one corner of the garage. It had taken them four long, hot trips around the neighborhood to haul everything home.

"You know what I think? I think we should space it out, pick up some of the stuff each day instead of trying to collect everything once a week," Marcy said.

Lisa looked at them both, her face twisted with worry. "If you want to back out on this deal, it's okay. I'll understand."

Kim stood up and faced Lisa squarely. "Will you stop that?" She hooked three fingers over each hip in the secret sign. "We wouldn't do this if we didn't want to."

"Right!" Marcy seconded.

Lisa gave them a tremulous smile. "You really mean it?"

Marcy nodded. "Nobodies stick together, remember?"

"What we need to do," continued Kim, "is divide up the houses, a few for each day, and take notes around telling people when we'll be there to pick up."

Marcy licked her lips, giving Kim a serious look. "You know something else we need to do? We need to elect officers."

Forgetting her train of thought, Kim stared, bewildered, at Marcy. Lisa looked puzzled, too.

"Officers?" Lisa said at last. "There are only three of us. Why do we need officers?"

"Think about it. A Secretary, a Treasurer—and a President.

*President.*

Kim had never been President of anything in her life. She felt excitement stir in the pit of her stomach.

*President of the Nobodies.*

To be the President would make her feel good inside, as though she were Somebody.

The three girls eyed each other. Kim sensed a change in the atmosphere, a tension which hadn't been there before.

Marcy smiled. Kim didn't like that smile. It looked sly.

"Treasurer is obvious," said Marcy. "Since Lisa is the one we're collecting the money for, she should be the Treasurer."

Kim thought she saw a look of disappointment cross Lisa's face. Did Lisa want to be President, too?

"That's a good idea," Kim said quickly. "Yes, Lisa, you should be Treasurer."

She flicked a quick glance toward Marcy and caught her friend doing the same with her. Their eyes met

92

uneasily. Kim turned toward Lisa and saw her staring down at the floor. Lisa seemed very quiet. After a moment she straightened her shoulders and looked up again.

"Okay, I'll be Treasurer," she said.

Kim sighed with relief. That left the offices of Secretary and President, and she knew she was the logical choice for President.

"Kim, you have the best handwriting, so you should be Secretary," said Marcy.

Shock shot through Kim's body as though she had stuck her finger in a light socket. She couldn't believe it! Marcy was actually trying to get the office of President for herself!

Oh no, you don't! Kim told her silently.

Aloud she said, "You draw better pictures than I do, Marcy. Those pictures of smiling pop cans on your handouts were really cute, and we'll need pictures on other handouts, too. You should be the Secretary."

Marcy surveyed Kim with narrowed eyes. It was as though the air crackled between them, Kim thought, like lightning in a storm.

"Handwriting is more important than drawing if you're Secretary." Marcy turned to Lisa. "Isn't that right?"

Lisa squirmed around, her face miserable. "I, ah—well, I don't know. . . ."

Kim's heart picked up its beat. She found herself breathing faster. "Of course you know. Marcy drew those cute smiling pop cans. . . ."

"You're a better speller than I am," Marcy interrupted. Her eyes shone brightly and she again wore a sly

93

smile which set Kim's teeth on edge. "You have to be a good speller to be Secretary."

"We'll just have to vote," Kim said. "I vote for you, Marcy, for Secretary."

"And I vote for you," replied Marcy.

Slowly both girls turned toward Lisa. Underneath, Kim felt triumphant. Lisa would vote for her. Hadn't she been Lisa's first friend, back when Marcy still thought Lisa was stuck-up?

Lisa twisted her hands together. "Well, I—I think you'd both be good either as Secretary or President. Um, it's hard to choose. But . . . Kim, you *do* have better handwriting. You should be Secretary."

Kim gasped. She felt as though Lisa had struck her right in the mouth. For a moment she couldn't breathe. She looked toward Marcy and saw a slow grin spread over Marcy's fat face.

Betrayed. She'd been betrayed by the two people she'd considered her best friends. The injustice of it filled her with such anger that she jumped up and ran into the house, slamming the door behind her.

When she reached her room, she threw herself down on the bed and pressed her face into the pillow. How could they! Maybe they'd planned it between them ahead of time. Maybe Marcy had given Lisa something, maybe even paid her, to get her vote. Her chest felt tight, as though a fist were slowly squeezing around her lungs. When she heard a knock on her door, she shouted, "Go away!"

"Hey, Kim." It was Marcy's voice outside the door. "Hey, Kim, can we come in?"

"No."

94

The door opened.

"Hey, Kim." It was Lisa. "Listen, I'm sorry. I didn't know—I really didn't know how much you wanted to be President."

"Anyway," interrupted Marcy, "we just took another vote, and you're the President now."

Kim lay very still, absorbing Marcy's announcement. Deep inside she felt a stirring of shame. She'd thought Joanne's behavior had been bad when the little girl had grabbed the wig while screaming, "Mine!" Now she could see she'd just thrown a tantrum, and she was eleven years old, not two. Suddenly she felt so embarrassed she wished she could die.

"Did you hear us, Kim?" asked Marcy. "We said you're the President now."

She felt hands on her shoulders.

"Hey, Kim, are you okay?" There was real concern in Lisa's voice.

Kim sat up. "I—I don't know what got into me just now."

"Anyway, we've made you President—" Marcy began, but Kim interrupted, shaking her head.

"I don't deserve it now, not after that scene I just pulled. And I *do* have better handwriting."

Marcy shook her head in turn. "I don't deserve it, either. I did know you wanted to be President, but I wanted that job, too, so I used the thing about the handwriting to make Lisa choose you."

"And I just threw a tantrum like a baby. Marcy, you be President."

"No, I couldn't, not now. I wouldn't feel right about it. You go ahead and take it."

"I wouldn't feel right, either—"

"I'll tell you what!" interrupted Lisa. "*I'll* be the President. And since I'm a pretty good speller, too, I'll be the Secretary. *And* the Treasurer. How's that?"

Startled, both girls turned to stare at Lisa. Looking a little sheepish, she grinned. "Just thought that might be one way to stop the argument."

Suddenly the whole thing seemed ridiculous. Kim slid off the bed and put her arms around Marcy. "I'm sorry."

"So am I," said Marcy, returning her hug.

Kim glanced toward Lisa. "Are you sure you still want to be friends with two Nobodies like us?"

"Where else would another Nobody fit in so well?" asked Lisa.

The two girls held out their arms, taking Lisa into the huddle. After a moment, Lisa spoke, sounding muffled with her head against Kim's arm. "We still don't have a President."

Giggling, the other two pushed her away.

"All right, what do you suggest?" Marcy asked.

Lisa picked a scrap of paper out of the wastepaper basket. She put her hands behind her back for a moment, then held out both fists in front of her.

"The one who picks the hand with the paper in it is the President," she announced. She waved her fists tantalizingly up and down.

"You go first," Kim said, hoping Marcy wouldn't pick Lisa's left hand. She had a prickling sensation in her own left arm which made her think that "left" was the correct choice.

"No, you go first," Marcy insisted.

Kim reached toward Lisa's left hand, thinking, Okay, Marcy, you had your chance.

Then she hesitated. Slowly, hoping she'd guessed correctly about the paper being in Lisa's left hand, Kim tapped Lisa's right hand. After a suspenseful pause, Lisa opened that hand to show that it was empty.

"Oh!" gasped Marcy, covering her mouth in surprise.

As she looked at Marcy's shining face, Kim felt a warm glow spread through her veins. She found herself laughing happily. She had never realized before that losing could feel good.

Patting Marcy on the shoulder, she said, "Congratulations, Madame President."

# Chapter 12

Once the girls got organized, they were able to settle into a routine: gymnastics three times a week, exercising and jogging every day, collecting the papers and cans each evening, keeping records for the club, as well as doing their daily chores at home.

Although Kim had never been so busy before in her whole life, she found that she enjoyed it. She even began to look forward to each gymnastics class. By pretending that the high beam was a board lying in the grass, she could move back and forth without teetering. Eric and Tish had started teaching the bar and beam routines, getting ready for the meet, and Kim had proved to be one of the better girls on beam. She could do most of the tricks, such as a scale, where she balanced on one leg while leaning forward and extending the other leg backwards. She sometimes lost her balance on the backward roll and had to be helped by Tish or Eric, but she was getting better at that, too.

"Beam's your event, I can tell," Tish said one day

after Kim had gone all the way through the routine without being spotted.

Later, Marcy said, "You look really graceful up there, Kim."

Sometimes, catching a glimpse of herself in the floor exercise mirror as she went into a pose on the beam, Kim thought it might be true.

Marcy's prediction that she'd never be able to do the squat-over vault again proved to be wrong. Whenever she charged down the runway and hit that springboard, the pop could be heard all over the gym. Her weight seemed no handicap as she soared onto the horse and touched it briefly with her hands to lift into the air for the off-flight.

Because Lisa concentrated so hard on bars, she soon made that her best event. She could even do the mill circle, where she scissored the low bar, then rotated forward all the way around to the top of the bar again.

"I'm no longer afraid," she told Kim and Marcy. "I know Eric will catch me if I start to fall. I just wish I could tell my mom about it."

One day, Jay Jay watched Kim do the beam routine. After Kim had finished, Jay Jay said to her, "You're looking better, but I'm still going to win the All Around ribbon in the meet."

"What's that?"

Jay Jay shook her head and rolled her eyes up as though Kim were really stupid. "That's the top award, dum dum! Your scores for each of the four events are all added together, and the girl with the highest total score wins first in All Around."

To win first in All Around! Kim caught her breath at

the idea as she turned to look toward the wooden boxes which were pushed back against one wall. The boxes could be fitted together to make a pyramid, with places for the winning girls to stand. For a brief moment she pictured herself standing on the top step while Eric announced, "And now, Kim Turner, our top All Around gymnast!"

Jay Jay waved her hand in front of Kim's face. "Hey, you still with us? What's going on?"

Kim blinked her eyes, refocusing on the present. "Nothing, I was just thinking about something."

Jay Jay peered at Kim shrewdly. "I know what it was. You're thinking about winning All Around."

Kim stared back in awe. Could Jay Jay read her mind?

Jay Jay grinned. "You were thinking that, weren't you! Well, you can just forget it, because *I'm* taking that All Around ribbon."

Eric had divided the class into two groups, with one group working on the floor routine with Tish while the second group worked on the beam routine with him.

"Okay, time to switch!" he called. "My group move to floor, Tish's group move to beam."

He walked off toward the floor mat without looking back.

Jay Jay made a disgusted face. "I didn't get my last turn on beam. It's not fair."

"He just forgot, that's all," Kim said.

"Well, I don't like getting cheated out of a turn," Jay Jay replied, her face stormy.

Kim shrugged and followed Eric toward the floor, then realized that Jay Jay wasn't with her. She turned to

**101**

see that the red-haired girl had climbed up on the beam and was going through the routine by herself. Kim slid her eyes toward Eric. She knew he wouldn't like Jay Jay to be up on the high beam without a spotter. Should she tell him? She didn't want to be a tattletale. On the other hand, what if Jay Jay fell and got hurt?

She looked again toward the beam. Jay Jay was getting ready for the hitch kick. Just then Eric turned and saw her. He ran toward the beam with his arms held out, but he was too late. At that moment, Jay Jay's foot slipped off the beam and she hurtled to the mat, landing in a heap with one leg crumpled under her body.

She won't be hurt, Kim thought. The mat's too thick.

But Jay Jay didn't get up. Instead, she leaned forward and gripped her right ankle.

"Ohhhh!" she moaned.

Eric knelt and gently pried Jay Jay's hands away from her ankle. He began examining the foot and leg from all directions.

"Doesn't seem to be broken," he announced at last, "but you've got a nasty sprain."

He picked Jay Jay up and carried her to the bleachers, then hurried to the refrigerator behind the desk and returned with an ice pack which he draped around the ankle.

"Just sit there with your foot up," he told her. "The ice will help keep the swelling down."

Jay Jay looked so pale that Kim began to feel sorry for her. She also felt guilty. If she'd told Eric the minute she saw Jay Jay up on the beam, maybe he could have gotten there in time to catch her.

The other girls clustered around the bleachers to watch

Eric doctor Jay Jay, and Kim edged forward to join them. When Eric had finished arranging the ice pack, he stood up and surveyed the class, his face stern.

"You see what happens when you don't wait for a spotter?" he said grimly. To Jay Jay he added, "I'm sorry you're hurt, but it's your own fault for disobeying the rules. If you ever get up on the bars or high beam again without a spotter, you're out of this class, and you're out of this gym." He flicked his eyes back toward the other girls. "That goes for the rest of you, too."

Jay Jay started to cry. "I'm sorry. I won't do it again."

"You certainly won't do it for at least a week, maybe two weeks," he replied, "because that ankle will take time to heal."

Kim shivered, gripped by mixed emotions. She did feel sorry for Jay Jay, but she also felt glad, just a little, that Jay Jay had gotten hurt. Jay Jay had acted superior to everyone else for so long.

*Pride goes before a fall.*

One of her mother's favorite expressions. In the past, Kim had paid little attention to the words. Now she thought about them while wondering how she could feel sorry for Jay Jay and glad at the same time. She felt guilty about feeling glad. It was all very confusing.

"All right, the rest of you, back to work!" Eric commanded.

Kim started to follow the others back across the gym. Then she stopped.

"I'm sorry about your ankle, Jay Jay," she said.

**103**

Was that a lie? No, she really was sorry, despite all those other feelings.

"Thanks, Kim," Jay Jay replied. She looked truly grateful for the sympathy.

Now feeling proud of herself, Kim started to walk away. Because her nose was in the air she didn't see the edge of the floor mat. Suddenly she stubbed her toe on the edge of the mat and sprawled forward on her hands and knees. Along with the giggles of the girls nearby, Kim could again hear her mother's voice: *Pride goes before a fall*.

She felt her face burn as she picked herself up.

"Hey, you gotta watch where you're going," Eric called.

Kim nodded, grinning sheepishly. She hated it when her mother's stupid sayings proved to be right.

# Chapter 13

One day Eric suggested that any girl who owned a tape recorder might like to make a tape of the floor routine music to work with at home.

"Scott's boom box has a built-in tape recorder," Marcy said later. "So how do we get him to lend it to us? Tackle him, grab it, and run?"

Kim laughed without humor. "You saw how well that worked before."

But the more she thought about making a tape of the music, the better the idea seemed. When she found Scott in the garage tinkering with the lawn mower, she decided to ask him straight out.

"Hey, Scott, I need to make a tape of the floor routine music. Can I borrow your radio?"

"No way."

"Please?"

"Nope."

So much for that, thought Kim glumly as she walked away.

That night at dinner, her father said, "If I'd known

105

how many cans and papers you girls were going to be storing, I might not have agreed to let you use our garage.''

Kim's stomach clenched in alarm. Was he telling her she'd have to move everything out?''

''Yeah, they've conned me into helping them haul all that stuff to the recycling center,'' Scott put in. ''It's gonna take several trips. I think they should split their profits with me, don't you?''

Kim peered anxiously back and forth between her father and brother. Slowly they both began to grin. Kim sighed in relief when she realized they were teasing her.

''Really? You'll have to make several trips?'' Kim's mother asked. When Scott nodded, her mother turned to her. ''Kim, we've always made your brother pay for the gas he uses. If it's going to be a number of trips, I think you girls should reimburse him.''

''Right!'' Scott put in quickly, still grinning.

Kim could see that was the only fair thing to do.

''I'll have to check with our Treasurer—'' Alarmed, she bit off the words. Her family wasn't supposed to know about the club.

Scott picked up on it at once.

''Your *Treasurer?*'' he hooted. ''Just how much money do you expect to make off this recycling stuff, anyway? And what are you gonna do with the loot when you get it?''

Kim bit her lower lip, furious with herself for what she'd said. She didn't want to—she *couldn't*—tell her family about the Nobodies, not after taking a blood oath.

**106**

"That's a good question," her father put in. "What *are* your plans, Kim?"

He looked just like Scott at the moment, Kim noted, with his unruly cowlick and his mischievous green eyes.

Still Kim sat in silence. How could she get out of this without telling a lie?

Her mother leaned forward and said, "Look, Kim, since your father is letting you put all that junk in the garage, he has a right to know what's going on. I'm getting curious, too."

Kim took a deep breath. "Well . . ."

Although she made no mention of the Nobodies, she suddenly found herself pouring out the whole story about Lisa's problems: how Lisa had made the promise to her father to take gymnastics, how her father had died, how her mother then got so sick . . .

As she talked, she realized she had her family's total attention. Even Scott had laid aside his fork to listen.

"So—so that's why we're collecting all this stuff," she ended. "We're trying to help Lisa make enough money to stay in the class."

She saw the other three members of her family exchange glances. They looked so serious that Kim got worried. Were they mad at her? Did they think she and Marcy were doing something wrong? Well, at least she hadn't told them about the Nobody Club—she'd kept that secret.

When her mother got up and walked toward her around the table, Kim shrank back, thinking maybe she was going to get a lecture. To her surprise, her mother wrapped her in a big warm hug.

**107**

"Honey, I'm so proud of you." Her mother's voice was husky as though she might be close to tears.

"Me, too," her father seconded.

Scott didn't say anything. When her mother stepped back, Kim peered toward Scott's chair and saw that he was gone. Soon he returned and plopped the boom box down by her plate.

"Can't let you get all the credit for good deeds in this family," he said gruffly.

"Oh, Scott, thank you!" Kim jumped up and tried to hug him, but he dodged out of the way.

"Take that, you villain. And that!" he cried, dancing around her while chopping the air with an imaginary sword.

She could see he didn't want her to go all mushy on him, but she couldn't help the warm glow which spread through her entire body. She'd never received this much support from her family before. She decided the troubles of the Nobodies were over.

But on Saturday morning, when the three girls had finished loading the station wagon for the first trip to the recycling center, Kim's worry returned. There were not as many papers as she'd thought. Just one more trip after this, that's all they'd have to make. Lisa and Marcy looked worried about it, too, but Scott seemed to think they had plenty of papers.

"Look how that back end is dragging!" he complained. "We're gonna ruin the shocks."

The three girls crowded in beside him for the ride. He drove very slowly, taking each bump or pothole at about five miles an hour.

**108**

When they reached the recycling center, Mr. Lewis came striding out to meet them.

"Hey, Lisa, I haven't seen you for a while! Thought you'd quit."

"No, sir," she replied. "We just decided to wait until we had a full load."

He laughed, peering into the rear of the station wagon. "I'd say you succeeded. Okay, take out the cans and put them on that scale over there. Then drive your car onto this platform here, and we'll weigh the car and papers together. We'll empty the car and weigh again, and I'll pay you the difference in weight."

That seemed like a clever way to do it, Kim thought. When they finished, Mr. Lewis said, "I'll get your money for you."

Lisa stopped him. "Not yet. We have to go back for a second load. Just keep track of everything and pay us all at once."

"A second load!" Mr. Lewis exclaimed. "You *have* been busy."

Driving home, reloading, and driving back took almost a full hour.

"Scott's sure being nice." Marcy whispered. "What's the matter with him?"

Kim shrugged, not wanting to reveal that she'd talked about Lisa. "Must be something he ate."

After they'd finished weighing the second load, the girls waited anxiously while Mr. Lewis figured the total.

"I think you're gonna break the bank," he commented with a grin.

But when he announced the total, Kim realized with a sinking heart that they were short of their goal. After all that work! And the next payment to the gym was due on Monday.

"Five dollars. We still need almost five dollars!" Marcy murmured when they were back in the station wagon.

Lisa nodded her head in despair. "I know."

"Maybe if you asked Eric, he'd give you an extra week to earn the rest of the money," Kim said.

Lisa sighed. "But that would leave us even shorter next month."

"Hey. Hey, you guys," Scott called over his shoulder. "Whatever you need this money for . . . well, how about if I lend you the five dollars? You don't have to pay me back right away."

A wave of love for her brother swept over Kim. He hadn't told he knew about Lisa! He'd actually realized how important it was to her for him to keep his mouth shut. In the past he'd been such a pest, teasing her, messing up her hair. Now she could see there was hope for him yet.

"I—we'd really appreciate it," Lisa replied. "But—well, we don't want to be in debt."

Scott shrugged. "Now listen, you dirty rats," he said in his James Cagney voice. "If ya don't pay up, I'll be comin' to get ya, see?"

Kim laughed. "It's okay, Lisa. Scott knows he'll be paid back. It's not like I'm going anywhere. Sooner or later he'll collect."

"With interest," Scott put in quickly. "I don't expect to have to clean my room for the rest of the summer."

But Kim didn't mind that he'd said that. There seemed to be some kind of unspoken communication going on between them. She could see he'd thrown that last part in to keep the others from suspecting how much he knew.

That Monday, when the other girls turned in their money for the class, Lisa was able to do so, too.

But that afternoon, after they'd finished practicing in Kim's backyard with the tape they'd made of the floor routine music, Lisa said, "Look, I've been thinking. I'm going back to collecting cans off the streets, along with our regular collecting. If I don't—well, I'll just fall farther and farther behind."

"We'll help," said Kim.

"Sure will," echoed Marcy.

By the end of the week, however, they had collected only four additional sacks of cans. As they stood looking glumly around the garage, Marcy said, "We're doomed."

Kim nodded, her spirits at the bottom of her shoes. She feared that Marcy's prediction just might be right.

# Chapter 14

Jay Jay had ended up on crutches for almost two weeks. She started working out again on a day when Eric was having the girls concentrate on beam and bars. Kim could see that the period of inactivity had put Jay Jay behind. Meanwhile, the girl in class who seemed to be forging ahead was Laurie Jones.

"All right, class, you'd better watch out for this one. She's lean and mean," Eric joked after Laurie threw a strong set on bars.

Laurie flashed a good-natured grin toward her class-mates as she ran to the back of the line. Her orange-and-rust-colored leotard brought out the coppery highlights in her glowing brown skin. Kim thought she looked beautiful.

"You've got to keep your toes pointed and your legs straight," Eric chided after Lisa had finished. "You could be good on bars if you'd tighten your muscles and get rid of those stops."

Looking crestfallen, Lisa trotted to stand behind Laurie. Laurie turned around and said, "That's okay, hon, you'll do better next time."

We're becoming a team, Kim realized. Just like Eric wanted.

It made her feel good and prompted her to say, after Jay Jay had failed to get all the way through the bar set, "Don't worry, Jay Jay, you'll do all right."

"I'd better," Jay Jay replied in a determined voice, "because I still intend to beat the rest of you and win All Around."

Well, almost a team, Kim amended to herself.

"I heard what Jay Jay said. She makes me sick," Marcy said later to Kim and Lisa as the class moved over to the beam.

Anne Everett went first. Despite her short, stocky build, the blonde girl seemed to have a good sense of balance which helped her stay on the beam during difficult moves. And Jay Jay, obviously trying extra hard after her failure on bars, did a routine which earned her a pat on the shoulder from Eric.

But Kim couldn't seem to stay on. After she'd slipped for the third time, Eric said sternly, "Kim, you have to concentrate."

"Well, this sure wasn't one of our better days," Kim observed to her two friends when they were getting dressed.

She felt depressed. How could they ever get ready for the meet? And how could they earn enough money to pay Scott back and still keep Lisa in class?

On Saturday morning, Kim's mother handed her a slip of paper and said, "I forgot to tell you yesterday. You had a phone call while you were at class. You were supposed to call this lady right back."

"Oh, great," muttered Kim when she saw the caller had been Mrs. Colbert. The woman had become one of the Nobodies' most enthusiastic can and paper savers. What if she'd decided to quit?

Filled with foreboding, Kim dialed Mrs. Colbert's number. When the woman got on the phone and heard Kim's voice, she said, "I needed to reach you yesterday."

"I'm sorry," Kim replied. "What is it, Mrs. Colbert?"

The woman's next words came as a surprise. "I need your help. I need it today."

Kim's nerves flashed with alarm. "My help? What can I do?"

"Okay, here's the story," Mrs. Colbert said, "I've been telling all my friends and family about what you girls are doing. And guess what?"

"What?"

"Well, Linda, my married daughter, called yesterday to say she's just rented a bigger house, and the people who moved out left the garage full of old newspapers. She has to get those papers out of there this morning because the movers are bringing her furniture this afternoon, and she has to put some stuff in the garage. Can you get over there and pick up those papers right now? Because if you can't, she's going to have to pay somebody to haul them to the dump."

A bubble of joy expanded inside Kim.

*A garage full of papers!*

"Tell me the address. We'll be right there."

Kim motioned frantically to her mother for a pencil. While she was writing down the address, Marcy and Lisa walked into the kitchen. Kim threw them an excited smile to show them something good was happening.

**115**

"Thank you very much, Mrs. Colbert."

"Thank *you*," the woman replied. "I'll call my daughter to say you're coming, and she'll be waiting there for you. God bless."

"Yahoo!" Kim yelled after she'd hung up.

"What is it?" Marcy demanded.

"You'll never guess!"

"You just won a million dollars in a sweepstakes?"

"Nope."

"Some guy asked you out on a date?"

"Of course not, silly. Guess again."

"Stop playing games! Tell us!" Lisa cried, grabbing Kim's arm and giving her a shake.

"Okay, okay."

After Kim had explained her news, the other girls let out excited whoops of their own.

"Let's go right now," Marcy exclaimed.

"Wait a minute," Mrs. Turner interrupted. "Don't you remember, Kim? Your dad took the station wagon to work today, and Scott's off hiking with a friend."

"Oh, no!" groaned Lisa. "What'll we do?"

The three girls sank down at the kitchen table and stared unhappily at each other. Mrs. Turner joined them.

"Marcy, couldn't you ask your father to help you just this once?"

"John's not my father—" Marcy began, but Mrs. Turner interrupted, speaking more harshly to Marcy than Kim had ever heard her before.

"He *is* your father, Marcy. He's adopted you. That makes him legally your father, just as much as Harry ever was."

Harry. Marcy's natural father. Kim knew her mother

**116**

had never liked Harry. Still, she felt her mother had no right to interfere in Marcy's life. She tried to give her mother a warning look, but Mrs. Turner paid no attention.

"Harry left you and your mother five years ago," Mrs. Turner went on, "and he's never been back to see you, not once. Frankly, I don't think you're being fair to John."

Marcy's face turned red as Mrs. Turner talked.

Kim could no longer keep quiet. "Mom!"

"Well, I see Kim wants me to shut up," Mrs. Turner said matter-of-factly, "and I guess she's right, this is really none of my business. But, Marcy, I've seen you hurt John, the way you ignore him. He takes good care of you, and he does love you, no matter what you believe. Think about it."

She got up and walked briskly out of the room.

Marcy sat with a stunned expression on her face while Kim squirmed with embarrassment.

"I'm sorry," Kim said. "She shouldn't have talked to you like that."

"Is John really terrible?" Lisa asked sympathetically. "Does he hit you or yell at you?"

"Well . . . no," Marcy admitted, "but I know he hates me."

"How do you know that? What does he do?" Lisa asked again.

"He doesn't *do* anything," Marcy replied. She sounded annoyed by all these questions. "It's just that he . . . well, he hates me, that's all. Joanne is the one he likes. I mean, she's really *his*. And she's pretty, and she wins prizes. While I . . . well, I'm a Nobody, you know that!" She stood up and faced them defiantly, her hands on her hips. "I'll ask Mom if she'll take us, but I won't ask John."

They found Marcy's mother baking pies.

"Ask your father to take you," she said.

"He's not my fa—" Marcy began, but caught herself just in time when Mr. Doyle walked into the kitchen.

Standing well over six feet tall, with thick brown hair and a lean-jawed, unsmiling face, he did seem frightening to Kim. Nevertheless, he agreed to take the girls at once after Marcy had timidly explained.

The Doyles did not own a station wagon. All they had was a family car. Looking it over, Kim hoped it had a big trunk.

When they reached the address Mrs. Colbert had given them, they saw a young woman standing in the driveway. She was dressed in jeans and a red T-shirt.

"Hi!" she called as they climbed out of the car. "I'm really glad you could come. I'll open the garage and you can see what I've got here."

As she pulled up the big double doors, the girls rushed forward eagerly to peer inside. Then all three jarred to a halt, crying, "Oh!"

Almost the whole garage floor was stacked knee-deep in newspapers.

"Good grief!" exploded Mr. Doyle.

The young woman grinned. "You see what I mean. The former tenants left all this here, and I have to get it emptied out by this afternoon."

Kim fearfully eyed Mr. Doyle. "It'll take a lot of trips."

He nodded and set his mouth in a firm line. "Let's get started."

**118**

They filled the trunk, the backseat and the back floor. Marcy squeezed in on top of the papers, which meant that Kim and Lisa had to sit with Mr. Doyle in front.

"Keep track of the mileage," Kim told him. "We'll pay you for the gas."

He looked surprised but didn't comment. In fact he had little to say during the whole morning. It took twelve trips back and forth to the recycling center to empty out the garage. Kim's father would have joked around and kept everyone laughing the whole time, but Mr. Doyle seemed to be the strong, silent type. Nevertheless, he didn't once complain, which Kim found amazing after the way Marcy had always run him down.

When they were putting the last of the papers into the car, Mrs. Colbert's daughter handed Kim a ten dollar bill.

"We can't take that," Kim said quickly. "We're selling these papers, you know."

"I know, but I would have had to hire someone to haul all this off if it hadn't been for you, and that would have cost me a lot more. You've done me a big favor here."

"No—no, it wouldn't be right," Marcy said, supporting Kim.

The woman took the bill and handed it to Mr. Doyle. "Then at least let me pay for part of the gas."

"The girls have said they'll pay for the gas out of the paper money," he told her. His voice was flat. Kim could not tell how he really felt.

"Why, I won't hear of it!" the woman cried.

"Actually, I'm donating the gas for today," Mr. Doyle went on. "I'm happy to help my daughter."

He didn't sound happy. But Kim was beginning to think that one couldn't tell with Mr. Doyle. Maybe he was a person who couldn't show his emotions. Maybe he really did care for Marcy, but she'd been reading him wrong all these months.

When they'd weighed the last load at the recycling center and Mr. Lewis had computed the total, he said with a wide grin, "You want to hear how much this comes to?"

When he announced the total, the girls jumped up and down, hanging onto each other for joy.

"I think they're happy," Mr. Doyle commented flatly to the air. But Kim saw one corner of his mouth lift ever so slightly. She decided he was smiling.

When they got home, Kim and Lisa said, "Thank you, Mr. Doyle."

Marcy added coolly, "Yes, John, thank you very much."

The man looked at Marcy for a long moment. Finally he nodded and went into the house.

Kim had the feeling he'd been waiting for something else—she wasn't sure what. Whatever it was, she didn't think he'd gotten it.

# Chapter 15

The girls immediately paid Scott back the five dollars they owed him. With the money they'd be making from their regular daily collections, they could see that they no longer had to worry about paying Lisa's bills for the rest of the summer—the garage full of newspapers had given them the extra boost they'd needed. Now they could concentrate on getting ready for the meet.

*The meet.*

Even Kim's toes tingled whenever she thought about it. There would be an audience, Tish had repeated. And *judges.*

Each girl would be out there *alone,* in front of everybody, doing her routines while the judges took off points for the things she did wrong.

"I'll probably wind up owing them points," Kim predicted darkly to Marcy and Lisa. "What if I forget and just stand there, looking like a fool?"

Marcy shivered. "Don't mention such a thing! I'm scared enough as it is."

"Remember to stretch," Tish kept repeating. "Reach

for the ceiling. Extend every muscle. And *point your toes.*"

That seemed to be one thing all the girls kept forgetting to do.

Tish was studying to be a judge and knew all about the deductions.

"You start with a score of ten," she said, "but every mistake lowers your score. If you bend your knees when they're supposed to be straight, that's a deduction. If you fall off beam or bars, that's a deduction, a big one. If you don't stretch, or point your toes, or if your hair is messy—those are deductions. If you mess up the routine and do stuff in the wrong places, or take extra swings on bars, or wobble on the beam, or hold your hands wrong—points off. When you're through, the judges add up all your mistakes and subtract from ten. What's left is your score."

"Probably a big fat zero," Marcy whispered to Kim.

Nevertheless, the Nobodies continued jogging and exercising every day to grow stronger.

One afternoon, when they'd paused to rest, Kim casually glanced at her two friends and then did a double take.

"Marcy, stand up," she commanded.

Looking puzzled, Marcy obeyed. Kim rose and circled around her.

"Hey, you've lost weight!"

Lisa jumped up and circled Marcy, too.

"You have, you really have."

Marcy looked down at herself. "I thought maybe I had, but I've been afraid to check."

"It's not only what you've lost, but you've . . . well,

**122**

you've shifted around what's left," Kim said. "Maybe because we're together every day I hadn't noticed before, but your flab's gone."

"Flab!" Marcy interrupted sarcastically. "Thanks a lot."

"Don't get mad," Lisa said hastily. "You *were* flabby before, but not now. No kidding, Marcy, you're looking good."

"Oh, dear," sighed Kim, glancing down at her own legs. "I've always been too skinny. If I've lost any more weight—"

"Your turn," Marcy said. "Just shut up and stand there."

The other two girls now circled around Kim. She watched their faces, trying to pick up their reactions. When Marcy finally shook her head, Kim's heart sank.

"I can't believe it," Marcy murmured.

"How bad is it?" Kim asked nervously.

The other girls began to grin.

"You've gained," said Lisa.

*"Gained?"* Kim exclaimed in disbelief. She twisted around, trying to look at her whole body.

"You've filled out," Lisa went on. "You've got muscles now."

Marcy nodded. "She's right. Even the calves of your legs—they're bigger now, so your knees don't look so funny."

"You're saying I had funny knees?" Kim asked fiercely. But she grinned so they'd know she was kidding. Underneath, she was feeling good.

"Okay, Lisa, your turn," she said.

But as Kim and Marcy walked around Lisa, Marcy

wrinkled her nose in disgust. "You were perfect before, and you're still perfect. I can't stand it."

Lisa's eyes filled with tears. "I don't feel perfect."

"What's the matter, what's wrong?" Kim asked in alarm.

"It's—well, it's my mom. Keeping all this about the gymnastics a secret from her . . . that's almost like an out-and-out lie. If I'm going to be in the meet . . ."

Kim punched her on the arm. "What do you mean, *if*?"

Lisa shook her head in misery. "I can't do it unless she knows. So I decided this morning, I'm going to tell her. I guess it might as well be today." She paused, looked from one girl to the other. "I really dread it. Will you both come with me?"

The bottom dropped out of Kim's stomach at the thought. She remembered that strange pale face in the tower window, the face she'd thought was a witch.

She glanced toward Marcy and read on her friend's face the same mixed emotions she was feeling. But when Marcy nodded slightly, Kim said, "All right, we'll come."

The three of them turned at once and headed down the sidewalk in the direction of Lisa's house.

# Chapter 16

When they drew near Lisa's house, Kim saw that it looked as spooky as ever. She imagined what the inside would be like: dark shadows, creaking stairs, cobwebs hanging in the corners.

Her steps began to drag. The other girls started walking slower, too. They climbed the porch steps to the front door, then stopped, staring at each other.

"I don't have the nerve," Lisa said.

"Do you want to back out?"

"Yes."

Just then the front door squeaked open. Kim jumped at the sound. She expected to see the same gaunt face which had been at the upstairs window. Instead, she found herself looking into the plump, pleasant face of a white-haired woman wearing a flowered apron over a blue housedress.

"Lisa, you've brought your friends! I'm so glad," the woman said, beaming a welcome smile.

"Grandma, this is Kim and Marcy," Lisa said. To her friends she added, "This is my grandma."

Marcy giggled. "We guessed."

The woman laughed, too. "You can call me Grandma if you want to, but my name is Elsie Faubion. I'm Lisa's mother's mother."

She stepped aside, holding the door open as the girls entered the hallway. While Lisa led the way into the living room, Kim looked around with eager curiosity. There were no cobwebs. In fact, the house appeared to be spotlessly clean. Because of its old-fashioned, narrow windows, it was darker than Kim's own home. Still, it seemed to be a cheerful place, with paintings on the walls, books on the tables, bright carpets on the floors, and, in one corner, a white wicker plant stand covered with African violets. An aroma of hot cinnamon and sugar spiced the air.

"Come on out to the kitchen," Mrs. Faubion said. "I've just baked cookies."

Marcy groaned.

"We're all on diets," Lisa hastily explained.

"You've got to be kidding," her grandmother responded. "Skinny little things like you?"

"That's the first time anyone called me skinny," Marcy replied.

"Grandma, do we have any apples?"

"Sure, honey, but don't you want at least one cookie?"

Kim sniffed again at the sugary smell and found her mouth beginning to water.

The three girls looked at each other.

"Just one?" Marcy asked in a pleading tone.

"Surely one couldn't hurt," Lisa put in.

"Okay," Kim agreed, glad that the other girls had talked her into it.

The kitchen turned out to be the happiest room of all, with a beamed ceiling, knotty pine walls, and a huge rag rug on the floor. There was a table in the middle of the room covered with a red-and-white-checked cloth. On the table sat a platter holding a pile of cookies cut in different shapes: stars, hearts, fish, rabbits, chickens.

"Take your pick," Mrs. Faubion said, waving one hand toward the platter.

Kim selected a star, while Lisa and Marcy each took a heart. Kim bit one corner off the star, chewing slowly to make the hot, spicy flavor last.

"Ummmmm," murmured Marcy, rolling her eyes in ecstasy.

Mrs. Faubion poured herself a cup of coffee and then selected a fat chicken cookie.

"I'm sure glad I'm not on a diet," she said. "I love to cook, and I love to eat."

Kim found herself thinking that Lisa's mother could not have come to a better place to get well.

*Lisa's mother.*

Suddenly Kim lost her appetite. She finished the cookie just to be polite.

When Lisa had swallowed her last bite, she asked, "Grandma, is Mom up in her room?"

A shadow seemed to cross the older's woman's face. "Yes, she's been taking a nap."

"Do you—do you think she'd like to meet my friends?"

Mrs. Faubion gave Lisa a tremulous smile. "Honey, I think it would do her a world of good."

Lisa set her mouth in a tight line of resolve. Slowly,

**127**

she nodded her head at her friends. "Well, I guess this is it."

A shivery feeling ran down Kim's arms. She and Marcy followed Lisa out into the hallway and up the stairs. The treads creaked beneath their feet. As Lisa turned the corner at the landing, the light streaming through a round stained-glass window framed her in an eerie glow.

Upstairs was a long hallway with three doors on either side. Lisa paused at one of the doors and rapped gently. Kim heard a faint voice call, "Come in."

When Lisa pushed open the door, Kim looked past her shoulder to see a slender woman with dark hair lying on a bed. The woman was dressed in black slacks and a black blouse. Lisa entered the room and motioned the girls in after her.

"Mom, I'd like you to meet my friends, Kim and Marcy."

Mrs. Andrelli sat up hastily and began smoothing her hair with her hands. Her face was thin and pale. There were dark circles under her eyes, just as there had been circles under Lisa's eyes when the girls had first met her. But Lisa had a good tan now, from all that jogging in the sun.

"You didn't tell me you had company," the woman said. Her voice sounded weak, as though she didn't use it much.

Kim glanced quickly around the room at the carved wooden bedstead, the old-fashioned dresser, the rocking chair. On a lamp table beside the bed sat a framed photograph of an extremely handsome dark-haired man

**128**

with one arm around Lisa, the other arm around Lisa's mother. They were all laughing into the camera and looked very happy.

Lisa's father, Kim decided. Her heart ached as she thought of his tragic death.

"Mom." Lisa swallowed hard. "Mom, I have to tell you something."

Mrs. Andrelli rose quickly from the bed. "What is it? Has something happened to your grandmother?"

"No, she's fine. She's downstairs baking cookies."

Mrs. Andrelli placed one hand against her chest over her heart. "You frightened me, you looked so serious."

"I, ah . . . Mom, I've been doing something this summer I haven't told you about."

Mrs. Andrelli sank down on the edge of the bed as though her knees had gone weak. "Are you in some kind of trouble?"

"Mom!" Lisa made a face. "Of course not!"

Mrs. Andrelli kept her eyes fixed on Lisa's face with such intensity that Kim felt uneasy. The woman looked as though she might break at any moment.

Lisa took a deep breath. "Do you—do you remember how Dad made me promise I'd take gymnastics this summer?"

Mrs. Andrelli frowned.

Lisa continued quickly. "Well, I felt I should keep that promise, so—so I *have* been taking gymnastics. I didn't tell you because I was afraid you'd worry."

Lisa's mother covered her face with her hands. Lisa glanced toward the others as though seeking their help, but Kim didn't know what to say. Finally Lisa went on

**129**

with her story, explaining about the class and about Eric's emphasis on safety.

"That's right, Mrs. Andrelli," Kim added, finding her voice at last when Lisa had finished. "He catches us if we fall. . . ."

She broke off, remembering that Lisa's father had been killed in a fall.

"Does your grandmother know?" Mrs. Andrelli asked, taking her hands from her face.

"No."

"Then how have you paid for your lessons?"

Smiling eagerly, Lisa explained about the recycling project and the money they'd made.

"You've done all that? Just the three of you?"

"Yes."

"Without asking me to help you?" The woman looked bleak. "I haven't been a very good mother lately, have I?"

"It's okay, Mom. I know you've been having a hard time."

"It's not okay. But I—I just can't seem to pull myself together. . . ." Mrs. Andrelli's voice faded away.

"There's one more thing," Lisa went on. "The gym is having a meet in about two weeks. I'm in it, Mom. I'll be in all the events. Will you come and see me?"

Mrs. Andrelli's shoulders sagged. She bent her head, staring at the floor. "I haven't been anywhere in a long time."

Lisa knelt beside her. "It would mean a lot to me. Please come."

"I don't know." She lifted her eyes to stare past Lisa's shoulder in an unfocused way, as though she were looking at something invisible to the rest of them. "I'll think about it. I just don't know."

"Thanks, Mom." Lisa gave her mother a hug. "The gym's only a few blocks away."

"And the meet won't last very long," Kim put in.

"Our mothers will be there, too," Marcy added.

"I haven't said I'll come," the woman protested. "I just said I'll think about it. Lisa, try to understand."

Lisa sat back on her heels. "Okay, Mom, I'll try. But you try, too. I need you."

Lisa stood up and led the girls from the room. Once they were back downstairs, Lisa leaned against one wall and let out her breath in a long sigh. "I'm glad that's over. But I'm glad I told her."

"Maybe your grandmother can talk her into coming to the meet," Kim said. "Let's go see."

They found Mrs. Faubion waiting for them in the kitchen.

"I just told Mom something which upset her a little," Lisa confessed. "I guess I'd better tell you, too."

Quickly, she filled her grandmother in on the story. At the end her grandmother reached out and patted her hand.

"You're a brave girl and I'm proud of you. Try to be patient with your mother."

Lisa nodded.

"Well, I can tell you one thing," Mrs. Faubion went on. *"I'll* be at that meet with bells on, you can count on it!"

Later, as the girls were leaving, Kim saw Lisa glance wistfully toward the stairs. Watching her friend's face, Kim hoped with all her might that Lisa's mother would

131

pull herself together in time for the meet. She couldn't help thinking how her own parents had never missed one of Scott's football games. Soon they would be coming to the gym to watch her perform for the very first time. It made her a little nervous, thinking about that, but it made her feel good, too.

She was lucky, she decided, that she had parents she could count on.

# Chapter 17

Eric and Tish stepped up the training program to get all the girls as well prepared as possible. Excitement began to fill the air during each class period.

Kim now knew most of the girls in class fairly well. Laurie Jones continued to be one of the better gymnasts in all events. Anne Everett wasn't too good on bars and floor, but her beam routine and her vault both looked strong. And Beth, the brown-haired girl whose last name, Kim had finally learned, was McNeil, had turned out to be one of the stars on floor.

"I've been taking jazz dancing and ballet for four years. That really helps," she'd explained one day after Kim had complimented her.

Then there were the two Chavez twins, Maria and Theresa, known as Merry and Terry. They were strong in all events, while a girl named Robin Henderson had proved to be one of the best at keeping her legs straight and her toes pointed on beam and bars.

Kim could see that Jay Jay was getting worried about winning first in All Around.

"We're going to hold the meet on a Saturday," Eric announced one day. "That way, more fathers can come."

Both Lisa and Marcy looked down at the floor when he said that. Kim felt sorry for Lisa but she didn't feel sorry for Marcy. She'd decided she agreed with her mother that Marcy was being unfair toward Mr. Doyle.

Some days Kim looked forward eagerly to the meet; other days she got scared, thinking about it, and wished it were over with.

One day in the gym she got distracted by some girls laughing nearby and walked right off the end of the beam into the air. She landed on her hands and knees on the mat.

"Kim, you have to concentrate," Tish scolded. "When that meet comes, you can't let anything distract you. Not the noise of the crowd. Not the judges. Not anything. You have to shut out everything else but your routine and you have to concentrate the whole time on what you're doing."

Kim began to have nightmares again. In one dream the beam was a mile long and there were judges lined up on either side for the entire distance. She could hear people booing in the background, while Tish yelled, "Con-cen-traaaaate!"

One morning, she woke up with a fluttery feeling in her stomach. She turned over, wondering if she were getting sick.

Then it hit her. The meet. The meet was *today!*

She jumped out of bed and ran in her pajamas to the kitchen where her mother was cooking breakfast.

"The meet's today!" she yelled.

Her mother laughed. "I know that. We all know that. You've been reminding us of it all week."

Her father put his coffee cup down on the kitchen table and laid aside his newspaper. "Kim, come here."

He sounded very serious. Kim went at once to stand beside him.

"What is it, Dad?"

"Look, honey, I'm sorry," he said, reaching out to touch her arm. "I won't be able to make it today."

Kim felt her knees go weak. "Can't make it? Why not?"

"Business isn't so good right now, and I've had to let one of my clerks go. I've got to work all day. We're in the middle of inventory."

"But, Dad! You—"

"Kim, please try to understand," her mother interrupted.

"But you've never missed one of Scott's football games, not ever!" Kim burst out. "If Scott were in a game today, you'd go, no matter what!"

"Don't be impertinent," her mother responded automatically.

"Well, it's not fair! You don't love me, you just love Scott!"

Her father's brows drew together in a frown. "That's not true, Kim, and you know it. I do love you, but I have to work today. I'm sorry, I really am, but it can't be helped."

He turned and walked out the door to where his car was parked in the driveway. Kim stood there in shock, still not believing the way things could suddenly change. Her mother came over and touched her hand.

"Honey, I know you're disappointed, but your father's right, he can't help this. If the store fails, we're all in trouble. I told you several weeks ago, I may have to go back to work, too."

**135**

"Mom—"

"Now be quiet and pay attention. We've got financial problems right now. I think we can handle it, but we need your help and cooperation. Yours and Scott's. Because we're all in this together."

When her mother put it that way, Kim felt better. "What can I do?"

"If I do get a job—well, I'll have to turn part of the housework and cooking over to you."

Kim nodded.

"But that's in the future," her mother went on. "Scott and I will be at the gym this afternoon. He says he's going to yell 'Go, Kim!' whenever it's your turn."

"Oh, no." Kim eyed her mother in alarm. "Please, ask him not to do that. He'll make me nervous."

She had a horrible vision of her brother rushing out onto the floor mat to muss up her hair. And Tish had said messy hair was a deduction.

Her mother laughed. "He's kidding. I think. But you know Scott." She gave Kim a quick hug. "Thank you for understanding."

She picked up some soiled dishes from the table and headed toward the sink. Kim hurried after her.

"I'll do that, Mom."

Her mother gave her a smile which warmed Kim clear through. "Another time I'll take you up on it, but today's your special day. You concentrate on the meet."

*Concentrate!* Tish's voice echoed in Kim's mind, and she grinned.

"Mom, you sure?"

"Yes. Now sit down and I'll cook you a good breakfast."

**136**

But just then Kim glanced out the window toward Marcy's house and saw a red piece of paper pinned to Marcy's curtain. Their special sign. Marcy needed help.

"I'll be back in a minute, Mom. There's something I have to do first."

She darted down the hallway and out the front door, then slipped around to the alley and through the bushes to the clubhouse. She entered to find Marcy pacing the floor and looking glum.

"What's up?"

"I'm so nervous I could die. An audience . . . everybody out there watching us . . . I'll fall and make a fool of myself, I just know it. Aren't you nervous? What if you mess up in front of your folks?"

Kim took a deep breath, then lifted her chin. "My dad's not coming to the meet."

Marcy's eyes got wide. "But he's never missed one of Scott's games."

"He has to work today."

"Well, if that isn't the pits!" Marcy plopped down in one of the chairs. "Me, I've got just the opposite problem. John *is* coming to the meet."

"That's good."

"No, that's bad. He's just coming because Mom's making him. I know that's the reason. He loves Joanne, not me."

*But he does love you!* Kim wanted to shout.

Then she shifted uncomfortably, remembering how she'd just accused her own father of not loving her when he'd proved his love for her many times. Like letting her store all those newspapers in the garage.

Unlike Lisa, she did have a father. And unlike Marcy,

she had a father who joked sometimes and made her laugh. He had said he was sorry. . . .

"Marcy."

"Huh?"

"About our dads. Maybe we should both lighten up."

"He's *not* my dad," Marcy began, but Kim didn't want to hear it.

"Look, I gotta get home and eat, and then wash my hair," she interrupted. "Since we have to get there early for warmups, shall we ride our bikes and let our families come together later? Scott and Mom'll be the only ones in the station wagon, so there'd be plenty of room for your folks and Joanne."

"But—"

"But seriously, we gotta forget about everything else and *con-cen-traaaate!*"

Marcy shook her head in mock disgust. "You're a nut."

"The nuttiest."

Marcy grinned. "Nutty Nobodies."

"That's us." Kim felt tingles of anticipation run down her spine. "In just a few hours the meet starts. The meet! With judges!"

Marcy's grin vanished. "We're doomed."

# Chapter 18

Kim and Marcy arrived at the gym an hour early. Already some of the other girls were there warming up, including Jay Jay.

"So you came. Thought you might chicken out," said Jay Jay. She looked them up and down with scorn. "Still wearing the same old leotards, I see."

Jay Jay had on a brand new leotard in white and navy blue. Her red hair was braided around her head in a shiny crown secured with white and blue ribbons. She looked gorgeous.

*But we look okay, too,* thought Kim, sliding her eyes toward Marcy.

The black leotard became Marcy more than ever, now that she'd lost weight, while the red one with the two pink stripes still looked good on Kim. Marcy's hair, shining clean, lay smoothly in place, held by the barrette with the pompoms. Kim's bangs, neatly trimmed, fringed her forehead, and she had curled her hair earlier to make bouncy ponytails over either ear, which she'd tied with red ribbons. She had on new white footies which felt cushiony under her feet.

She had eaten little lunch, not wanting to weigh herself down with heavy food, and she was so keyed up that she had twice as much energy as usual.

I feel good, she thought. I feel lean and mean.

The girls jogged laps and then stretched before taking turns on the equipment. Lisa showed up in her green leotard. She had an excited smile on her face.

"Mom's coming!" she announced. "She told me just before I left."

Kim hugged her. "That's great! When she sees how safe this gym is . . ."

"Just watch me fall off today, and watch Eric miss me," said Lisa.

Marcy socked her lightly with a fist. "Don't say it. Don't even think it."

The crowd began to gather, filling the bleachers along one wall. When Lisa's mother and grandmother arrived, the girls ran to greet them.

"Where are your bells?" Kim asked Mrs. Faubion.

She responded with a jolly laugh. "I forgot those, but I can whistle through my teeth."

"She can, too," Lisa confirmed. Turning to her mother, she asked with concern, "How are you doing, Mom?"

Her mother took a shaky breath. "I'm not sure."

"Don't you worry about her," Lisa's grandmother said firmly. "You just concentrate on what you have to do."

Kim laughed. "You just said the magic word. *Concentrate!*"

The girls went back to the workouts. Kim glanced

toward the clock on the wall. Only ten minutes before the meet was to start. Where were her mother and Scott? Where were the Doyles?

Then the door opened and they all trooped in. Despite the fact that Kim had known her father wasn't coming, she still felt a stab of disappointment when she saw he wasn't with the group. She realized then that subconsciously she'd been hoping he'd make it after all.

"Hi, Mawcy!" called Joanne. Dressed in yellow shorts and a ruffled yellow shirt, with a big yellow bow covering her damaged hair, she looked like a dancing sunbeam.

Again the girls ran to greet the newcomers. When Scott reached out a hand as though to ruffle Kim's hair, she growled, "Don't you dare!"

Then she led her mother over to meet Lisa's family. She was pleased when her mother sat down beside Mrs. Andrelli and started drawing her into a conversation.

"Okay, girls, line up!" called Eric. "Time to begin."

He arranged the class members in a row according to height. "After the National Anthem, go sit on the low beam over there against that wall and wait for your name to be called for an event," he said. "Remember, if you mess up, no tears! Salute the judges each time and march proudly back to your seat. Good luck!"

All of a sudden, Kim found that her mouth had gone dry while her palms had become sweaty. But when the music started for the parade around the mat, she held her head high. And when Eric announced, "Laaadies and Gennntlemen, greet your gymnasts!", Kim's heart swelled with excitement as the audience applauded.

After the National Anthem, Eric introduced the judges. He said that there would be only two judges for a meet this small, and he explained that their two scores for each event would be averaged together to give the final score for each girl.

The first judge he introduced was a Mrs. Andrews. She was young and pretty, and she smiled at all the girls. But the other woman, Mrs. Schultz, looked mean. She had gray hair, thick glasses, heavy shoes, and a frown. When she looked the girls over, she pulled her brows together and clamped her mouth tight. And *she* was Head Judge.

"We're doomed," Marcy whispered in Kim's ear.

The girls moved to sit on the low beam.

"Vaulting first," announced Eric. And then he said something Kim had never heard before. "Lisa Andrelli is up, Anne Everett is on deck, and Kim Turner is in the hole."

"What does *that* mean?" Kim whispered to Lisa.

"I think it means I go first," Lisa said. "That makes you third in line."

Kim's stomach tightened nervously.

Lisa took her place at the end of the runway while Eric stood to one side of the horse, ready to catch her. He turned briefly to the audience.

"Each girl is allowed two tries at the vault," he explained. "The better vault is the one that counts."

Kim glanced toward the bleachers. Everyone there was watching eagerly except for Mrs. Andrelli, who had her hands over her eyes.

Lisa held up one hand in a salute, as Tish had taught them to do. Mrs. Schultz nodded in return, showing that the judges were ready.

Lisa took a deep breath, gave a little hop and loped

down the runway. When she hit the springboard, it gave a muffled pop, not the sharp explosive sound of a good leap. Her preflight was low and her feet were apart. Kim remembered that Tish had said those errors brought deductions. Nevertheless, Lisa managed to stick her landing without taking any extra steps. She stretched to a finish before turning and bowing to the judges.

While the audience applauded, the judges both began figuring rapidly on pads attached to clipboards. Eric spoke briefly to Lisa, then returned to stand beside the horse while Lisa did her second vault. This time she had to take two steps at the end to keep her balance. Again, Eric stopped her afterwards to say something. When she rejoined Kim and Marcy, she held out one hand to show how she was shaking.

"Eric says I need to hit that springboard harder," she whispered.

While Kim moved toward the end of the runway to await her turn, she kept an eye on Anne's first vault. It looked good. The second vault looked even better.

Then it was Kim's turn. She teetered on her toes at the end of the runway and looked toward the horse. It seemed to be a thousand miles away. Her heart pounded, her breath started coming fast.

When Mrs. Schultz gave her the go-ahead signal, Kim sped down the runway. But the second she jumped onto the springboard, she knew that she had made the same mistake as Lisa: she hadn't put enough force behind her jump. She tried to make up for her lack of momentum by pushing hard with her hands on top of the horse. Her arms gave way, tumbling her headfirst over

**143**

the horse toward the mat. Eric's arms grabbed her just in time while the audience groaned.

Eric stood her on her feet.

"Salute!" he commanded, stepping away.

Her face burning with embarrassment, Kim lifted her arms in the air and then turned to bow to the judges. Mrs. Andrews gave her a sympathetic smile, but Mrs. Schultz frowned as though Kim's vault had been a personal insult. The older woman then began making marks all over her pad.

I might as well quit right now, Kim thought in despair.

Suddenly she felt an arm around her shoulders.

"Here's where you went wrong," Eric said calmly. "Now listen, and avoid these mistakes on your next vault. Don't forget, it's the best vault that counts."

When he had finished his instructions, he gave her a pat on one arm for encouragement. Then he went to stand once more beside the horse.

While Kim took her place at the back of the runway, her mind seemed filled with voices. Her own voice: *You're a Nobody. No wonder you messed up.* Tish's voice: *Concentrate!* Eric's voice: *It's the best vault that counts.*

And then she heard Scott shouting from the stands, "Go, Kim!"

Her head snapped up. She searched the bleachers until she located her brother's eager face. He nodded at her, grinning as he held one thumb in the air.

Straightening her shoulders, Kim peered toward the horse and *concentrated*. When the judges gave her the signal, she still waited for a moment, focusing her whole attention on the coming vault.

**144**

When she started her run, she moved slowly at first, gauging the length of her stride. Then she picked up speed, hitting the springboard with all her might and popping into the air. She knew her preflight was good, but she felt her feet come apart as she headed off the horse. She landed off-balance and stumbled around for a moment before she could get her bearings. But at least she hadn't fallen on her head. After saluting the judges, she stepped from the mat.

"Much better," said Eric.

She heard the audience applaud as she trotted back to the low beam.

"That one looked pretty good," Marcy told her.

For the moment, Kim relaxed, watching the other vaulters. Jay Jay did well on both vaults. So did several of the other girls, including Laurie and Terry. Then it was Marcy's turn.

Marcy's first vault looked perfect to Kim. But on her second vault she lost her balance on the landing and fell forward on her hands and knees. She looked glum as she walked back to the other girls.

"Well, I just blew it," she said in disgust.

"Maybe not," Kim replied. "They score the better vault."

But Marcy shook her head. "I'll bet if you mess up on one, they think you're not very good and they count you down on both."

Kim couldn't answer that. She didn't know how the scoring worked, but she did know one thing: Mrs. Schultz hated them all and would take off for everything she could.

Bars came next. Terry Chavez was the first one up,

and she did very well. Marcy went second, but she fell off once and also took three extra swings.

"Well, I blew it again," she said to Kim after she'd finished. "I might as well go home."

Laurie Jones, looking trim in a yellow leotard, mounted the bars with clean grace. Although she paused a couple of times during the routine and took an extra step on her dismount, she gave a good performance.

Then Kim heard Tish announce, "Kim Turner is up, Beth McNeil is on deck, Merry Chavez is in the hole."

Bars had always been Kim's poorest event. This time proved to be no exception. At one point during the routine she lost her concentration and had to wait until she could remember what to do next. On the mill circle she bent her knees. In another place she used the wrong hand grasp.

"I think we both just blew it," she murmured to Marcy when she rejoined her friends. "This is terrible!"

Every now and then a girl at the head table flashed the scores, but Kim kept losing track of which score was for whom. She tried to tell herself that winning a ribbon wasn't important, that just getting through the meet was all that counted.

Who are you kidding? chided her inner voice. You want a ribbon, and you know it!

She heard Tish call, "Jay Jay Carr is up, Anne Everett is on deck, Lisa Andrelli is in the hole."

"Here I go!" Lisa said nervously. "Is my mom okay?"

Kim searched the stands with her eyes. Mrs. Andrelli had turned her head away, while Kim's mother seemed to be talking soothingly to her.

Jay Jay did an excellent job, but Anne Everett appeared heavy and slow.

Then Lisa approached the bars. Suddenly she stopped as though she'd run into a wall. She looked up at the high bar with all the color draining from her face.

Oh no! thought Kim. She's getting scared.

As Lisa stood there, the gym grew very quiet. Lisa's mother leaned forward and buried her face in her hands. Mrs. Turner put her arm over the woman's shoulder. Lisa shut her eyes, swallowing hard.

Kim couldn't stand it. She had to break the tension.

"Go for it, Andrelli!" she yelled.

Her words echoed around the gym. Some of the people in the stands looked toward Kim with disapproval. She knew they thought she was being rowdy. But Scott seemed to catch on to the fact that Lisa had frozen.

"Go Lisa!" he called.

Lisa opened her eyes, looking in misery toward the stands. Slowly, her mother lifted her head. She stared at her daughter for a long moment. Taking a breath, she called, "Go, Lisa!"

Lisa's face brightened as though a light had turned on behind it. Kim had never seen anyone change so suddenly from despair to joy. As Kim watched, Lisa lifted one arm high. But the salute was not for the Head Judge. With shoulders back, chin up, arm reaching for the sky, Lisa saluted her mother. As the two of them looked at each other, they both began to smile.

Still keeping her arm in the air, the girl stepped onto the mat. Briskly she saluted Mrs. Schultz.

"Look!" whispered Marcy, nudging Kim in the ribs.

Kim saw Lisa's thumb and little finger flare to either side, while the three middle fingers, pressed together, pointed toward the ceiling.

Kim caught her breath. *That* signal, she knew, was a salute to her and Marcy.

Lisa moved forward and mounted the bars, going at once into an aggressive routine. She had very few form breaks and she managed to keep her knees straight and her toes pointed. After zipping all the way through without a pause, she sailed into a strong dismount and snapped erect to salute the judges once more.

The crowd went wild with applause. As Lisa stepped from the mat, Eric flung his arms about her, lifting her into the air and swinging her around. When she trotted back to the other girls, both Kim and Marcy jumped up to give her an additional hug.

Kim heard a shrill whistle over the applause. Glancing toward the bleachers, she saw that Lisa's grandmother had two fingers between her teeth.

"You did it!" Marcy cried. "Lisa, that was great!"

Lisa exhaled slowly, shaking her head in disbelief. "I nearly froze up for a minute. Did you hear my mom?"

Laughing happily, Kim said, "We sure did, and we heard your grandmother, too."

When all the girls had completed bars, the judges rose to move their chairs toward the beam. As Kim glanced toward that narrow length of wood, she felt a shiver run down her arms.

Beam was her best event. If she was ever going to win a ribbon, then this would be her one chance.

Marcy turned out to be the first girl up. Beam was *not* Marcy's best event. Sure enough, she wobbled around during the routine as though her legs and arms had turned to wet spaghetti, and she fell off twice.

Kim saw both judges scribbling furiously on their pads. They figured for a long time and then held a conference before sending in their final score.

"So much for beam," muttered Marcy as she rejoined the others.

Eric came over to kneel beside the girls.

"Tough luck, Marcy," he said. "What you have to do now is forget beam and concentrate on doing your best when you get to floor."

Marcy gave him a grateful nod.

Kim thought it was nice the way Eric encouraged them, even when they did a poor job. She remembered how, when she'd first met him, she'd feared he might be mean. She knew now that he was a tough coach, but he really cared about his team.

Anne Everett went next. She did a fairly good routine, but she also fell off once. Laurie Jones fell off, too, and so did the Chavez twins.

Eric looked toward Marcy and laughed. "Must be catching," he whispered, "like chicken pox."

Then it was Jay Jay's turn. Kim watched with special attention. She felt that Jay Jay would be the hardest to beat on beam. Sure enough, Jay Jay approached the beam with confidence. She made her mount without any problems and swung into a smooth routine, performing each move in a sharp, clean way. Whenever she hit a pose, she stretched for the ceiling and held her chin high.

Kim's spirits sank. She knew there was no way she could equal that.

But on the last pass Jay Jay's foot slipped off the beam. She fell lightly to the mat and hopped right back on, proceeding through the dismount. When she rejoined the class, Eric greeted her with a big smile.

"That was excellent, Jay Jay," he said, "even though you did catch Marcy's falling bug before it was over."

Beth McNeil went next. She did well, and she managed to stay on throughout her routine.

Then it was Lisa's turn. Although her hitch kick was low, she kept her routine flowing in a steady rhythm. Her scale was wobbly, but she recovered and managed to stay on during the backward roll.

"Whew, I'm glad that's over!" she whispered to Kim afterwards.

Then Kim heard her own name called. All of a sudden, her pulse began to race. She took a deep breath, trying to calm down.

"You can do it!" said Marcy.

"Go for it!" Lisa chimed in at the same time.

This is it, Kim told herself. Now concentrate!

As she approached the beam, she glanced toward Mrs. Schultz, only to be met by a cold scowl. Her knees began to shake. She remembered her dream where everyone had booed.

She saluted and mounted the beam. Never had that length of wood looked so narrow. Gravity tugged at her from either side, pulling her first one way and then the other. She wobbled with every step. When she tried the hitch kick which she had done well in practice, she barely made it into the air before coming down again. Her feet felt like lead. She tried to stretch, as Tish had told her to do, but her whole body shook.

**150**

*Point your toes. Don't bend your knees. Hold the scale for two counts. The right arm is up, the left arm out. . . .*

Then it happened. Her foot slipped on a turn and she windmilled the air with her arms, tottering back and forth. The floor reached up with an invisible hand and jerked her right off the beam. She landed in a crouch on the mat.

*No tears.* That's what Eric had said.

Blinking her eyes, Kim forced herself back up on the beam. Halfway through the backward roll, she fell off again. That time Eric darted forward to catch her.

Nightmare. This is a nightmare, she thought in a panic as her stomach churned. How big a deduction would it be if she vomited on the Head Judge?

On the tuck jump dismount, she leapt into the air, tucked her heels up under her bottom, landed on slightly bent knees, straightened, and reached for the ceiling. That wasn't too bad—at least she didn't take an extra step. She saluted the judges, then hurried back to the low beam and sank down beside her friends.

"Are you okay?" whispered Marcy.

Kim made a face. "About as okay as if I'd just fallen off a ten-story building."

Eric came over and patted her shoulder. "Too bad, Kim. You caught the Marcy fever."

The look of chagrin on Marcy's face at Eric's continued joke made Kim smile in spite of herself. Still, she could not shake the disappointment which clung to her shoulders like a wet coat.

Eric knelt down beside her. "Kim, I know you're unhappy, but you've got to swallow it and go on. That's

**151**

the way gymnastics works. What you have to do now is concentrate on floor. Go for it!''

*Go for it.*

Kim looked up and met his eyes. He nodded firmly.

"Go for it," he repeated.

Kim felt her disappointment fade away. A seed of determination budded inside her and expanded throughout her body, giving her new strength. Floor was not her event, but maybe, just *maybe,* she could do okay out there if she really tried. Maybe not win a ribbon, but at least make her mom and Scott feel they had not come in vain.

Eric rose and walked over to the desk. "Jay Jay Carr is up, Beth McNeil is on deck, Kim Turner is in the hole," he announced.

Kim leaned forward and carefully watched each of the other girls go through their routines. They were the stars on floor, they were the best. As each of them performed, Kim kept reminding herself, Point your toes. Keep your knees straight. Stretch for the ceiling. Keep to the music.

If she could just remember all that. . . .

But when she marched out onto the floor mat for her turn, she felt her courage begin to waver. Her ears rang, her knees trembled.

"Go for it, Kim. You can do it!"

Scott's voice.

"Go, Kim."

Her mother.

And then a whole chorus of voices: "Hey, Kim!" "Go for it, Kim!" "Yay, Kim!"

The Nobodies were cheering her on!

**152**

She tightened her muscles and took a deep breath. Lifting her chin toward the ceiling, she took the opening pose. The music began.

*Step, step, turn, hop—*

She kept her toes pointed and concentrated on holding her arms just right.

*Body wave—*

She reached back, then swung her arms forward as she bent her knees and pulled her stomach in tight toward her backbone. She rose a little, then bent even lower and swung her arms backward while arching her torso forward. She felt the wave of her muscles flow right through her body from her ankles up to the top of her head until she was again standing on her toes with her arms stretched toward the ceiling.

*Step, run, split leap, run, cartwheel, cartwheel—*

The music seemed a part of her now, flowing through her and telling her what to do. She knew she was showing off, and Mrs. Schultz would probably count her down for it, but she no longer cared. All she wanted was to do a good routine for her mother and Scott so their afternoon wouldn't have been totally wasted.

*Step, kick, handstand, forward roll—*

It felt smooth, it felt *right*. A smile lifted the corners of her mouth. The gym, the audience, seemed to vanish. She was alone in the world of music and movement.

*Step, step, hurdle, roundoff—*

She punched the surface of the moon and lifted into outer space where gravity ceased to exist. Then she came down again and went at once into a backward roll.

*Up, turn, pose, chin high, arms curved.*

The music stopped, the moon vanished. Suddenly she

**153**

found herself back on Earth. Somewhere in the distance people clapped and whistled.

"Way to go, Sis!" shouted Scott.

Kim felt a big grin split her face. She saluted the judges, then marched back to her place, keeping her chin high. She'd done the best she could do. It wouldn't be enough to win a ribbon, of course, but at least Scott had seemed to enjoy it.

"Stay seated, please, for the awarding of the ribbons," Eric called.

Kim's elation vanished, and she swallowed against a sudden lump in her throat. One ribbon. If she could just have won one ribbon—

But it was too late. The events were over.

# Chapter 19

Tish and Eric moved the winners' steps to the middle of the floor. Then Eric walked over to the head table and came back with a cluster of ribbons in his hand.

"Before I announce these awards, I want to say that every girl here is a winner," he told the audience. "These routines are hard. The class has worked hard this summer, preparing for today. If you think you can do better, come out here and try it."

Everyone laughed at that, even Kim. Still, she wished Eric would just get it over with.

"Well, here goes!" He grinned, looking toward the girls. "In sixth place on vaulting . . . Beth McNeil!"

Beth jumped up with a pleased smile. While the crowd applauded, she loped out to take her place on the winners' steps.

"In fifth place . . . Terry Chavez!"

Both Terry and Merry let out excited squeals. Then Terry ran to the step marked "5" to accept her ribbon.

Kim's pulse began to pound. She slid her eyes toward Marcy and saw her friend sitting with her hands tightly clasped and a strained look on her face. If Marcy were to win a ribbon, this would be the event. But Marcy had made that one bad vault—

"In fourth place . . . Laurie Jones!"

Laurie leapt up and raced to the winners' steps. She smiled happily when Eric handed her a ribbon.

"In third place . . . Anne Everett!"

Marcy's shoulders slumped lower. Maybe it was true, Kim decided. Maybe that bad vault had cut down Marcy's score.

"In second place . . ." Eric paused longer this time.

Kim sent up a silent prayer that he would call Marcy's name.

"In second place . . . Jay Jay Carr!"

Kim felt physically sick. She touched Marcy's arm, trying to comfort her.

"And our vaulting champion for today is . . . Marcy Doyle!"

"What?" Marcy's head snapped up in surprise.

Eric laughed and waved the blue ribbon. "Come on, Marcy, front and center!"

Kim felt a warm glow blossom in her midsection and spread all through her body.

"Marcy, you won!"

Lisa gave Marcy a shove. "Go for it, Doyle. Go pick up that blue ribbon!"

Moving at last, Marcy ran out on the floor and scrambled to the top step. When Eric handed her the blue ribbon, she hugged it gently, as though it might break.

The audience broke into loud applause. Mr. Doyle

left the bleachers to take a picture of the winners with his InstaPrint camera.

"My daughter!" he explained proudly to Eric as he motioned toward Marcy.

"Mawcy, Mawcy!" shrilled a piping little voice over the applause.

Kim looked toward the bleachers where she saw Joanne hopping up and down. Mrs. Doyle had one hand wound tightly in Joanne's shirttail. Otherwise, Kim could see, Joanne would be out there on the winners' steps, too. With a happy grin, Marcy waved her ribbon at Joanne.

Back on the low beam beside her friends, Marcy said, "Can you believe it?"

Kim reached out to touch Marcy's ribbon. It felt slick and cool.

"Bars next!" announced Eric.

Lisa gave a little shiver. Kim knew what was going through her mind. If Marcy had won a ribbon, maybe she had a chance, too.

"In sixth place . . . Terry Chavez."

Again the sisters squealed together, making the audience laugh. After Terry had accepted her ribbon, Eric asked the audience, "Are you ready for this? In fifth place . . . Merry Chavez."

With a whoop Terry left the winners' steps to meet her sister. They hugged each other, hopping up and down. Eric rolled his eyes and shook his head.

"You wouldn't think they'd have that much energy left. And now in fourth place . . ." He paused dramatically.

Lisa, Lisa, Lisa, Kim kept repeating to herself.

"In fourth place, Beth McNeil."

**157**

Kim bit her lip. She looked up and down the line of girls, trying to remember who had had the best bar routines. Jay Jay and Laurie had both looked good on bars. But then, so had several other girls.

"In third place, Laurie Jones!"

Laurie loped across the floor and took her place on the steps. Kim slid her eyes toward Lisa. Lisa met her glance and shook her head, showing she knew she wasn't going to make it.

"And now our second place winner on bars . . . Lisa Andrelli!"

Lisa's breath exploded in a gasp of surprise. Again a shrill whistle split the air and Kim turned toward the stands to see that Mrs. Faubion had two fingers in her mouth.

"Yay, Lisa!" called her mother.

When Lisa had climbed to the step marked "2," Mr. Doyle stood up to take another picture. Lisa held up the ribbon and flashed her mother a big smile.

"Our bars champion, Jay Jay Carr!" called Eric.

Well, it was to be expected, Kim thought. Jay Jay had thrown an excellent bar set.

The strip of red silk gleamed brightly in Lisa's hand as she ran back to rejoin Kim and Marcy.

"Good for you!" cried Marcy.

She and Lisa placed their ribbons side by side on the bleachers so they could admire them. Kim felt a stab of jealousy. She wanted a ribbon, too.

"Now for the winners on beam!" called Eric.

Kim's pulse fluttered with excitement. Maybe, just maybe, she'd done better on beam than she thought. After all, beam was her best event.

"In sixth place on beam, Robin Henderson!"

Kim crossed her fingers and held her breath.

"In fifth place on beam, Anne Everett!"

Kim's eyes began to blur as the girls took their places.

"In fourth place . . . Lisa Andrelli!"

Kim's stomach clenched with pain. Lisa—a winner on beam? But that couldn't be. Beam was Kim's event, not Lisa's.

Through disbelieving eyes, she watched her friend run toward the winners' steps.

*Two ribbons for Lisa.*

She sat in a daze as Eric finished announcing the winners: third place, Laurie Jones; second place, Jay Jay Carr; first place, Beth McNeil.

Kim dug her fingernails into her wrist. She would not cry. She would *not*. There were a lot of other girls who hadn't won ribbons, either. Eric had said they were all winners, just for being in the meet. If she could hang on to that thought . . .

When Lisa returned with her yellow fourth place ribbon, Kim had to swallow hard in order to make her voice steady. "Congratulations, Lisa."

Lisa gave her a worried look. "Kim, I'm sorry. Beam's your event."

Kim shook her head, managing a smile. "Not today. Hey, it's okay, it really is."

But it wasn't okay. She felt sick with disappointment. Her one chance to win a ribbon had been on beam, and she'd blown it.

"Now for floor," said Eric.

Kim kept her head down, staring at her lap.

Just hold on, she told herself. It'll soon be over.

The two Chavez sisters again won ribbons, but reversed the order: Merry took sixth, and Terry took fifth. Laurie came in fourth, and Jay Jay took third.

Kim looked up in surprise. Jay Jay in *third* place on floor? How could Jay Jay be third? Kim had thought it would be a close race between Jay Jay and Beth for first place.

"Our second place winner on floor . . . ." Eric grinned, prolonging the suspense. "Our second place winner . . . Beth McNeil."

Kim frowned, looking up and down the girls who were left sitting on the low beam. Who in the world could have beaten both Jay Jay and Beth on floor? Who was left who was that good? No one.

Eric held up the blue ribbon. "And now our first place winner on floor . . ." He paused dramatically. "Kim Turner!"

Kim went numb with shock. There had to be a mistake. She could not have beaten Jay Jay and Beth. Eric had said the wrong name.

Then she felt Lisa and Marcy pounding her on the back.

"Well, don't just sit there like a dodo!" Marcy demanded. "Go pick up your ribbon!"

Kim rose unsteadily and stumbled toward the winners' steps. She heard the audience applauding, heard Scott yell, "All right, Kim!"

At last she stood on the top step, still dazed with shock. Eric laughed as he handed her the ribbon.

"Good job, Kim. You really showed that routine."

Beth leaned over from the second place step to give Kim a hug. "Congratulations, Kim."

"I can't believe I beat you, not on floor," Kim whispered.

"I'm okay at dance, but I need to work on my tumbling," Beth replied. She began to grin. "Next time, though, watch out! I'm gonna give you a run for your money."

*Next time.*

Kim felt a glow of excitement spread all through her body.

*Next time.*

Up until then, she hadn't realized there would be a next time. Now she knew, looking toward Marcy's and Lisa's shining faces, that somewhere along the way gymnastics had gotten into their blood. She felt sure that when the time came to sign up for the fall classes, the three Nobodies would be first in line.

When she rejoined her friends on the low beam, they both gave her big hugs.

"We all three got ribbons!" Marcy said, shaking her head in amazement.

"Time for the All Around winners," called Eric. "In sixth place, Lisa Andrelli!"

That time Kim felt nothing but joy as her friend accepted the orange sixth place ribbon. Quickly Eric ran through the rest: fifth place, Terry; fourth place, Merry; third place, Laurie; second place, Beth; and All Around Champion, Jay Jay Carr.

"That's it, ladies and gentlemen," Eric said. "Thank you for coming."

Kim and Marcy darted out on the floor to congratulate Lisa.

"Told you I'd win first in All Around!" Jay Jay gloated as she brushed by Kim.

Kim caught Beth's eye and grinned. "Congratulations, Jay Jay, but next time, watch out! I'm gonna give you a run for your money."

"That'll be the day," said Jay Jay.

Kim laughed. "Just wait and see!"

She joined Lisa and Marcy and the three of them hurried toward the bleachers. Kim's mother pushed through the crowd to give her a hug.

"I'm so proud of you. Your floor routine looked beautiful!"

Scott appeared beside them. "Great going, Sis," he said, reaching out to ruffle her hair. But Kim didn't care about the messy hair since Mrs. Schultz could no longer deduct for it.

As Lisa and her mother hugged each other, Mrs. Faubion announced emphatically, "It was my whistling that did it, I just know."

Kim watched Marcy approach her family. First Marcy hugged Joanne and then her mother, but her eyes were fixed on Mr. Doyle. There seemed to be a tension in the air that Kim didn't understand. She felt something was about to happen, but she wasn't sure what. Marcy took a step toward the tall man, then paused. They looked at each other for a long time.

"I'm so proud of you, Marcy," Mr. Doyle said at last. "You—you looked beautiful out there." There was a catch in his voice.

162

Suddenly Marcy darted forward and flung her arms around him. "Thank you, Dad."

The man leaned down, returning her embrace. "You'll never know how much I've wanted to hear you call me that."

Kim smiled. It had, she decided, been an excellent day.

# Chapter 20

The three families gathered near the gym door. Smiling happily, Marcy's mother said, "I have a huge pitcher of lemonade in the refrigerator at home. I wish you'd all stop by our house for a celebration."

Kim could tell that Marcy's mother was celebrating more than just the winning of ribbons.

Kim's mother turned to Mrs. Andrelli. "Please, will you come?"

Lisa's mother hesitated for only a moment before saying, "I'd love to."

"In that case," exclaimed Lisa's grandmother, "I have something out in the car I'd like to bring to the party. It's a big box of—"

"Cookies!" shouted the girls in unison.

The woman lifted her eyebrows in mock surprise. "How did you ever guess?"

The girls rode their bikes to Marcy's house. There they learned that Scott had already grabbed a cookie and gone on down to the store to help his father. The others had gathered in the kitchen to sip tall, cool glasses of

**165**

lemonade. The girls joined them there and spread their ribbons out on the kitchen counter like a bright fan. Five ribbons. For the Nobodies.

But we're no longer Nobodies, Kim thought. We can do all kinds of things, Lisa and Marcy and me. Maybe we always could. We just didn't know it.

She turned to look at the other people in the room: Marcy's parents with their arms around each other; Lisa's mother and grandmother laughing at Joanne's chatter, with Kim's mother joining in; Marcy and Lisa, her very best friends.

She thought of her father, working hard down at the store to take care of his family, and of Scott, who had rallied when she needed him.

Love for them all blew through her like a warm wind.

Everyone of them is Somebody in one way or another, she thought. I'll bet everyone in the world is Somebody, if they could only believe it.

After the others had moved into the living room to talk, the three girls slipped out the back door and ran toward their secret hideout.

We'll have to change our name, Kim thought. The Somebody Club? The Winners' Circle?

Her mind buzzed with plans. As she followed her friends through golden shafts of afternoon sunlight, she could still feel, flowing over and through her body, the wind of love.